W9-ABF-168

VOW OF ADORATION

By the same author

A Vow of Poverty
A Vow of Fidelity
A Vow of Devotion
A Vow of Penance
A Vow of Obedience
A Vow of Sanctity
My Name is Polly Winter
A Vow of Chastity
Last Seen Wearing
A Vow of Silence
My Pilgrim Love
Hoodman Blind
Flame in the Snow
Pilgrim of Desire
Echo of Margaret

A VOW OF ADORATION

VERONICA BLACK

St. Martin's Press ✄ New York

ONE

'I feel like a spare part,' Sister Joan said gloomily, giving Lilith a last stroke with the brush.

Lilith turned her head and uttered a low, sympathetic whinny. One of her front hoofs pawed the straw delicately as a hint that grooming was all very fine but she hadn't yet taken her exercise.

'Come on then, girl!'

Sister Joan reached up for the blanket and saddle, her small hands moving swiftly as she secured the harness. In the yard the glinting sunlight of early summer fell on the cobbles and slanted through the open kitchen door where Sister Teresa could be seen peeling a small mountain of potatoes at the scrubbed deal table. Though she was still only in her mid-twenties she exuded an air of calm security that had caused Sister Gabrielle to observe that the girl had clearly been born to fulfil the role of lay sister in life.

'Did you say something to me, Sister?' Potato peeler still in hand she appeared at the kitchen door, her lively dark eyes questioning.

'I was just telling Lilith that I feel like a spare part,' Sister Joan said, leading the pony out.

Any other sister might have uttered a polite disclaimer. Sister Teresa laughed and said frankly, 'I'm not surprised! It must be rotten not to have a particular job to do. Why don't you have a word with Mother Dorothy?'

'Mother Dorothy told me that for the present I'm to plug the gaps,' Sister Joan said wryly. 'In other words I'm the odd job nun!'

Sister Teresa grinned.

'At least it gives you a bit of leeway,' she said. 'I wouldn't mind a bit of a ramble across the moors myself.'

'And I shouldn't be grumbling,' Sister Joan said. 'I'll see you later.'

She swung herself astride, the ankle-length skirt of her grey habit flying up to reveal the denim jeans she wore beneath, a concession allowed by the prioress to preserve modesty. The short white veil covering her cropped black curls fluttered about a rosy face that looked younger than her thirty-nine years and was enhanced by a pair of dark-blue eyes fringed by long dark lashes that hinted at an Irish ancestor somewhere in her Lancashire family tree. She gathered up the reins, waved to Sister Teresa and trotted beneath the arch round to the front of the beautiful old building where once the Tarquin squires had lived and which now was the Cornish Convent of the Order of the Daughters of Compassion. Its façade was ivied; its long windows set in their mullions curtained plainly in white where once brocade had hung; its long drive still neatly raked between the low grass at each side but free from carriage wheels and the constant coming and going of visitors.

It was probably ungrateful of her, she mused, that she should feel restless because for the moment she had no definite job within the enclosure beyond looking after the pony and the young guard dog, Alice, who was still far too skittish to guard anything for more than two minutes, and filling in wherever an extra hand was required. The problem was that she sometimes felt that her own gift for painting wasn't being sufficiently utilized.

'When you can offer up your art for the glory of God and take no personal pride in it whatsoever, then we might be able to find a place for it,' Mother Dorothy had said.

And as there wasn't much hope of that happening yet, Sister Joan thought, she might as well stop feeling sorry for herself! She flapped the reins briskly over Lilith's broad back and urged the animal into a canter as they passed through the open gates on to the moor.

No finer site for a semi-enclosed Order could've been found than here, with the moors spreading around, a broad track leading southwards into the small grey town, the northern track leading to the rash of council houses beyond. Away to the west, the gaily painted vardos and clutter of the local Romanies were spread out along the banks of the river; to the east the moor became wilder, great chunks of rock rising up out of the surrounding moss and peat. Here and there on the horizon a solitary farmhouse stood.

It had been a wet winter and spring with rain falling in solid sheets and no chance of being able to give either Lilith or Alice their regular exercise. The turf under Lilith's hooves was spongy and bright green; every bush she passed shook off showers of sun-glistened raindrops in the breeze. Her mood lifted as she rode, and she found herself humming under her breath.

Brother Cuthbert, emerging from the little stone house which was also convent owned, used in the recent past as a school for the younger children, and now used as a convenient lodging for the young monk, raised a muscular arm and waved vigorously.

'Good morning, Sister Joan! Did you ever see such a marvellous day?' he exclaimed.

Since for Brother Cuthbert every day was a marvellous one Sister Joan merely nodded, pulling Lilith up and looking down with affectionate amusement at the aureole of bright ginger hair surrounding the gleaming tonsure.

'Are you off somewhere, Brother Cuthbert?' She nodded towards the rucksack on his back.

'I'm off to Scotland, Sister,' he told her.

'To Scotland!' There was dismay in her face. 'You've not been recalled to your monastery?'

'I was only permitted to come here for a sabbatical,' he reminded her.

'Yes, but – we all hoped that they'd forget about you,' Sister Joan said. 'Well, not exactly forget, at least not the way it sounds, but feel able to get on without you. You're very valuable here.'

'Really?' Brother Cuthbert's freckled young face brightened.

'It's very reassuring to wake up on a dark night and know that

Brother Cuthbert is only a couple of miles off keeping us all in God's mind,' Sister Joan said.

'Oh, I don't think that the dear Lord needs my prayers to keep Him up to scratch,' Brother Cuthbert said with a grin. 'But I'm not going for ever, Sister. My father superior wants me back with the community for a month. Then all things being well I'll be back here.'

'And naturally you'll be happy to see the other brothers again,' Sister Joan said.

'Whether they'll be so delighted to see me is another matter,' Brother Cuthbert said, with another irrepressible grin. 'I was never very much use in the community. Too absent-minded and clumsy you know. Anyway I was on my way down into town to leave the key with Father Malone for him to pass to Mother Dorothy. May I give it to you instead?'

'Yes, of course.' Sister Joan took the key and thrust it into her pocket. 'But you're not stealing away without saying goodbye surely?'

'It's only *au revoir*,' Brother Cuthbert said. 'I'll be back before you've missed me. Now I must be off. Father Malone has my train ticket so I'd better not keep him waiting. You'll give my regards to the community and say I hope to see you all very soon?'

'Yes, of course. Have a safe journey and return quickly,' Sister Joan said.

'Thank you. God bless, Sister!'

Brother Cuthbert shouldered his rucksack and went off, his sandalled feet sinking into the turf and causing small waterfalls of damp mud, a fact of which he was sublimely unaware since his eyes were fixed on the heavens again.

Sister Joan rode back towards the track and watched his figure diminish into the distance. It was odd but though Brother Cuthbert lived solitary and was seldom seen up at the convent she already felt an absence.

She wheeled Lilith about and set off eastwards to where the moors dipped and then swelled in long curves of peat and bracken and scrubby grass above the little town whose main street ran like a twisting grey ribbon off to the right.

Apart from the occasional farmhouse there were few signs of habitation here. The moors had retained something of their primitive wildness, wind and rain having carved the stones into grotesque shapes which, seen through the eyes of imagination, assumed the guises of trolls and giants and strange twisted crones reaching skywards.

She dipped down into a small valley through which a stream bubbled and pulled up Lilith before a low stone building almost buried in creeper, the roof half gone, the oaken door hanging on its hinges.

This was the first time she had ridden so far and the sight of the unexpected building roused her curiosity. It looked as if a chapel of some kind had once been its purpose, though it had been permitted to fall into disuse long before. Father Malone might be interested to hear of it.

She slid from the saddle and looked about for something to which she could tether Lilith. There were several thorn trees, stunted and leaning down towards the rain-soaked grass.

'Come on, girl!'

She looped the reins over the branch of one of the thorn trees and walked on into the building, picking her way carefully over small heaps of mud-encrusted pebbles that half silted up the doorway. An old building like this might well harbour wildlife. Birds and rabbits were welcome but she doubted if she could ever learn to love bats and rats, so kept her eyes fixed on the earth floor, alert for suspicious droppings. To her relief there didn't seem to be any and when she stopped to look up at the roof with its gaping hole and blackened beams she heard no betraying flutter of wings.

Half a dozen pews with sides higher than her head were ranged at each side of the unfloored aisle and nearer the entrance some rotting benches were piled up. Moss and lichen had encroached over the inside of the walls, and there was a dank, cold smell despite the breeze that blew the ends of the creepers into fantastic and tangled shapes.

'When Brother Cuthbert returns I'll tell him about this place,' she said aloud, and started slightly as her voice seemed to echo around her in a cascade of dying syllables.

There were no windows in the gaps in the walls and no sign of an altar at the eastern end. Perhaps it had been a Methodist meeting house, Methodism having struck its roots deeply into Cornish culture. On the other hand such buildings were generally well maintained. Stables perhaps at some date in the past? The pews would've made excellent stalls.

She paused by one and pulled open the door, the rusted handle cold and heavy across her palm. Within, the remains of a rotted seat designed to hold about five people held an abandoned bird's nest, its twigs sodden, its occupants flown.

She moved on, pulling at the next door, trying to imagine the local people who must once have sat here, the women in bonnets, the men in their Sunday black.

This pew wasn't unoccupied. A man wrapped in a greatcoat lay on what remained of the seat, head turned sideways, face beginning to bloat. The smell was very strong.

She had seen death before and it never failed to move her. Certain deaths horrified her and this was one of them. She hastily made the sign of the cross and stumbled out into the fresh air, retching.

Almost certainly a tramp had taken shelter there and died of natural causes. Sister Joan felt that she ought to go inside again and take a closer look but her courage and her stomach rebelled against it. Instead she wiped her mouth shakily with a tissue, unfastened the rein and remounted, forcing herself to breathe deeply of the damp, sweet breeze.

It was a long ride down into town. Somewhere around must be a farmhouse from where she could telephone. She rode up out of the hollow and scanned the landscape.

Across two fields of grain that had been planted in defiance of the elements, a long, low house hugged the further bank, its façade pebbledashed in white, its roof trimly green with a long plume of smoke waving welcome from one of the many chimneys.

The crop was sodden from the recent rain but was drying out, struggling upright, pale-green tips blowing in the wind. Sister Joan took the path that bisected the planted acreage, forcing herself to keep Lilith to a steady pace. There was no point in raising a panic when it was clear that nothing could be done. The poor man had been dead for at least a couple of days already. Haste couldn't help him now.

The gate at the far end of the second field was open. She rode through into the lane, then dismounted and led the pony through a second pair of gates into a curving drive which led between a series of shallow, flowered terraces towards the front porch.

There was a low rail before the front door to which she tethered Lilith before she went up the three shallow steps and rang the bell. It shrilled through the house and somewhere inside a radio was abruptly switched off.

Sister Joan stood back and waited. A curtain covering a bay window at the side was lifted and dropped. A moment later a chain rattled on the other side of the door and the door itself was opened a scant three inches.

'We're not Catholics here,' said the woman holding the door.

'I'm not collecting or anything,' Sister Joan said quickly. 'I wondered if I might use your telephone for a minute or two. I'm Sister Joan from the convent higher up across the moor.'

'Why would you want to use a telephone?' The woman's thin mouth was pulled tighter like a string closing a paper carrier bag. Above the thread of scarlet the eyes were cold and blue.

. 'There's been an accident down in the old chapel,' Sister Joan said, longing to stick her foot in the narrow gap between door and wall.

'Chapel? Oh, that place!' The woman looked slightly more forthcoming. 'In that case you'd better come in. That old place ought to be pulled down! I've told Mr Peter many a time!'

She had unlatched the guarding chain and opened the door to reveal a pleasantly sunlit hall with a staircase winding to the right and doors to both left and right.

'Your boots?' she said suddenly.

'Boots?' Sister Joan looked down at her neatly shod feet.

'Muddy!' the woman said, screwing up her face. 'I cannot have mud trodden into my clean carpets!'

'No, of course not! I beg your pardon!'

Sister Joan hastily knelt to untie her laces and set her muddy boots on the doorstep.

'Is that animal going to defecate on my doorstep?' the woman demanded, spying Lilith who gave her a look of indignant innocence.

'I can't guarantee anything,' Sister Joan said, her patience shredding, 'but I do know there's a worse stink down in the old chapel than Lilith can produce. May I please use your telehone?'

'You'd better come this way. I'm only housekeeper here so I have to be particular on account of it isn't my property,' the woman said.

'And you are—?' Sister Joan followed her through the nearest door, her socks sliding over the glossy parquet.

'Mrs Rufus. There's the telephone.'

They had entered a long sitting-room furnished in a slightly old-fashioned style with several pieces of what looked like genuine antique furniture arranged against the walls hung with a Regency striped paper in apricot and pale brown. The telephone was a modern one, set on a Queen Anne table with a thick, embroidered runner beneath it.

Sister Joan lifted the receiver and dialled the three nines. At the door Mrs Rufus said with reluctance in every bone of her angular body, 'I'll leave you to phone then. I'll be in the kitchen making some tea.'

Obviously she wasn't sure if nuns could be trusted with valuables. Sister Joan nodded, told the operator she wanted the police and a moment later was speaking to Constable Petrie down at the local station.

'Sister Joan! Nice to hear your voice again, Sister! Detective Mill's on holiday, I'm afraid, else I'd put you straight through to him. Everybody well up at the convent?'

'Yes, thank you. Constable, I'm telephoning from – I didn't notice the name of the house – but it's on the eastern slopes above an old building that looks like a disused chapel.'

'Does the house have a nice rockery in front of it?' Constable Petrie enquired.

'Yes. Yes it does.'

'That'll be Michael Peter's house. He owns the antique shop up in Croft Court.'

'I think I've seen it but I've never had occasion to go in.'

'Prices too steep, eh?' The constable chuckled. 'So what can I do for you?'

'There's a body in the old chapel,' Sister Joan said.

'Another murder?' Constable Petrie's slow Cornish voice had lifted and quickened hopefully.

'I hope not,' Sister Joan said fervently. 'No, it looks like natural causes. It's a tramp and I think he's been dead a couple of days. It's rather – unpleasant.'

'Can you meet us down there?' Constable Petrie sounded as if someone had just made him monitor of his class. 'I've got a couple of the lads here, but I'll need to leave one on the desk to take calls. Sergeant Bright went over to Penzance. Give me twenty minutes.'

The receiver at the other end was replaced. Sister Joan hung up, crushing down disappointment. If Detective Sergeant Alan Mill had been there she would have felt as if she had just handed over her problem to someone who would relieve her of all the responsibility concerning it. Alan would've collected her from the house and not left her to make her way back to the chapel alone. Alan Mill, she thought, with a little twinge of guilt, regarded her more as a woman than a nun. It was doubtless for the best that he was away on holiday!

She looked round the room again, her eyes appreciating the subtle blending of colour, the Picasso lithograph – surely it was an original – the trio of tiny ivory horses under glass on a side table which looked like genuine T'ang Dynasty. Mr Peter obviously knew his trade.

'I've brewed tea.' Mrs Rufus, looking marginally more friendly, possibly because she'd eavesdropped on the telephone call, reappeared in the doorway.

'Thank you. A quick cup would be very welcome,' Sister Joan said. 'May I make another very quick call first? To the convent.'

'I don't have to pay the bill!' Mrs Rufus said with unexpected skittishness and vanished kitchenward again.

Sister Perpetua answered the phone at the second ring,

doubtless on her way to or from the infirmary where the two oldest members of the community spent most of their time.

'Sister Joan speaking. I may be a little late home. Something came up.'

'Don't tell me you've found a dead body,' Sister Perpetua said.

'How did you—? You make it sound as if I'm always doing it,' Sister Joan protested.

'If you want my opinion,' Sister Perpetua's voice said crisply, 'you make a positive hobby of it! Not another murder, I trust?'

'A tramp. He looks as if he died of natural causes.'

'Poor fellow! May his soul and the souls of all the faithful departed rest in peace. I'll ask Sister Teresa to hold back your supper for fifteen minutes.'

The telephone was replaced. Sister Joan repressed a grin as she hung up at her end. Sister Perpetua, with her quiff of greying ginger hair escaping from her headdress, her large, flat feet and salty comments on life in general was a constant source of secret delight to her. Only old Sister Gabrielle could hold a candle to her when it came to quick wits.

She padded to the door and went into the hall again. Another door was open and the rattling of teacups guided her into a modern kitchen filled with gadgets, presided over by the housekeeper who indicated the chair opposite her own.

'Help yourself to milk and sugar,' she said, not unamiably.

'Thank you. I can't stay long,' Sister Joan said, accepting the chair and the tea. 'I have to ride back to the old chapel and meet the police there.'

'Not very nice for you,' Mrs Rufus said with unexpected sympathy. 'Mind, this is a lonely place. Mr Peter loves it up here but I'm always glad that I don't live in.'

'You live in town?'

'Over in the housing estate. I've a nice little bungalow there. Mr Peter picks me up in the morning and runs me home after he's had his supper. I don't drive.'

'He's a bachelor?'

'Until last summer.' The thin mouth became thinner again. 'Then he got himself wed. There was no need for it, no need at all! He'd managed very comfortably for forty-five years without a wife but you know what men are – or perhaps you don't, being a nun.'

'I know what men are,' Sister Joan said.

'A bit of a girl he met on his holiday.' Mrs Rufus sniffed. 'Not an educated girl, if you'll excuse my saying so.'

'But pretty?' Sister Joan guessed.

'Arty crafty,' Mrs Rufus said. 'Very sweet but not a brain cell working. She's away at present visiting her family so I can get on with my work and not have to listen to the latest pop songs blaring out all day long. More tea, Sister Joan?'

'I'd love some but I'd better go. Thank you again.'

'I cleaned your boots off a bit,' Mrs Rufus said, preceding her to the front door.

'That was very kind.'

'Well, seeing as the animal didn't disgrace itself,' Mrs Rufus said somewhat obscurely. 'Perhaps you'll let me know what happens? I'm here every day except Sunday from eight to eight. On the Sabbath I go to church – Low Church. I don't usually hold with a lot of fuss and ritual.'

She closed the door abruptly as if repenting of her former friendliness.

'Come on, girl!' Sister Joan tied on her boots and remounted, casting a final glance back at the house which stood looking incongruously smart and civilized with the moor and the few small patches of cultivated field all about.

She took her time to ride back through the ripening grain and was relieved to see a couple of police cars and an ambulance drawn up in the hollow, and Constable Petrie, wearing his unexpected authority with pride, as he issued instructions to a couple of junior constables.

'Good morning, Sister Joan!' His good-natured young face beamed with genuine pleasure as she dismounted. 'Very good of you to telephone so promptly. It's appreciated.'

'I thought it best to report the incident as soon as possible,' Sister Joan said .

'Ah! You and I understand the importance of these things, don't we, Sister? Time is of the essence when there's an unexplained death in the matter.'

'Is it unexplained?'

'The police surgeon is having a preliminary look now before the remains are removed. From the quick look I took I'd agree with you that the fellow probably took shelter in the old chapel and died there – hypothermia, heart attack, something of that nature. We shall find out soon enough. You didn't touch the remains?'

'No.' Sister Joan shook her head, grimacing.

'The clothes will be examined in due course. I'll let you know the results.'

'That would be very kind of you, Constable,' Sister Joan said meekly.

If Alan Mill stayed away for very long on his holiday, she thought, his constable would probably start planning his own autobiography entitled, *Cases I Have Solved, with the Help of Detective Sergeant Mill and Sister Joan*!! She said aloud, 'How are Mrs Petrie and the baby?'

'Both very well, thank you. The baby's walking and chattering fifteen to the dozen now. In fact the wife and I were thinking it was about time—' The constable broke off, his ruddy cheeks darkening.

'Time to go in for another?' Sister Joan said. 'Yes, that sounds like a good idea. Two children can play together and give their mother a bit of peace.'

'As you say, Sister. Now, can you just let me know why you were riding in this particular spot? It's a bit out of your way, isn't it?'

'I've never ridden so far this way before,' Sister Joan said promptly. 'Lilith needed the exercise and I was in the humour for a good gallop myself. You're not putting me down as a possible suspect, are you?'

'Just getting the facts straight, Sister.' Constable Petrie scribbled busily in his notebook. 'Ah, looks as if they've finished.'

A thickset man, pulling a medical mask from his face and stripping off surgical gloves as he came, approached them.

'Looks like natural causes but we'll know more later,' he said.

'We'll get the body down to the hospital now, Constable. Sister.'

He afforded her a brusque nod.

'Doctor Grigson.' Sister Joan nodded back. From his manner she would've guessed, if she hadn't known already, that he considered nuns should stay in their convents praying and not riding round getting mixed up in sudden death. 'Do you know how long ago he died?'

'Two – three days. We'll know more later. Are you going to rope off the area, Petrie?'

'The lads will have a close look over the building and then we'll wait for your report,' Constable Petrie said. 'I've had a couple of photographs taken. We'll need to identify the corpse.'

'Mid-forties, clothes shabby but of good quality, no marks of violence, no other distinguishing marks,' Dr Grigson said breezily. 'Doesn't look as if he's been on the road very long.'

'Thank you, Dr Grigson.' Constable Petrie made a note. 'Would you like to have a look round inside, Sister?'

'Not particularly,' Sister Joan said. 'I ought to be getting back.'

'Thanks for reporting the matter,' Constable Petrie said. 'No murder this time, eh?' There was a faint tinge of regret in his voice.

'Not this time,' Sister Joan said, moving to remount the patient Lilith, aware that without warning the sun had sped behind a cloud and a chill wind had begun to blow.

TWO

More than the allotted fifteen minutes delay had gone by when she led Lilith into her stall, removed saddle and blanket, and hurried through the back door. In the large kitchen with its two lay cells leading off it Sister Perpetua was just bending to the oven.

'On the Day of Judgement you'll be bringing up the rear!' she observed tartly. 'You'd best eat it here. The rest are at recreation.'

'It was very good of you to wait, Sister,' Sister Joan said, seating herself.

'I didn't wait on your account,' Sister Perpetua said. 'I've been at sixes and sevens since Mother Dorothy turned the timetable around. Supper at six instead of seven, an hour and a half's recreation instead of an hour and evening service at eight for two hours instead of one. I cannot get used to it!'

'You know it was agreed that going to chapel at eight would help Father on the days he comes to offer benediction,' Sister Joan said. 'And spending two hours in chapel instead of splitting it into an afternoon and an evening session does keep the day from being chopped up.'

'I'm sure you're right.' Sister Perpetua sniffed to demonstrate her private opinion of changes in the timetable. 'Personally I blame Vatican Two. Now tell me what kept you? You mentioned a body.'

'A tramp who apparently died of natural causes.' Sister Joan briefly retailed her mild adventure.

'Naturally you had to stay to report the matter to the police,'

19

Sister Perpetua admitted. 'You know you remind me of that film star – Elizabeth Taylor, is it? She made a charming film about Lassie. I saw it years ago before I entered the religious life.'

'I don't see the connection,' Sister Joan said, puzzled.

'She collects husbands and you collect dead bodies and, upon my soul, I don't know which is worse!' Sister Perpetua gave a dry chuckle at her own wit and put a small cake and a cup of tea on the table.

'I hope that people don't see me in those terms.'

Sister Joan's smile had wavered and she looked anxious.

'Nonsense, Sister, of course they don't!' Sister Perpetua patted her shoulder. 'I was only teasing you. Hurry up with your supper and then join the others at recreation. Sister Teresa and Sister Marie will be down in a moment to wash up.'

The extended recreation allowed the two lay sisters to join the rest of the community for an hour before they discharged their final kitchen duties. Only Sister Hilaria and her solitary postulant, Bernadette, left the main building after supper and walked through the grounds to the former dower house which was now the novitiate.

Sister Perpetua went out, large feet plodding down the corridor which led past the refectory and the infirmary where Sister Gabrielle and Sister Mary Concepta slept, on account of their age rather than ill health.

She finished her fish, ate the cake and drank the welcome cup of tea. At breakfast-time coffee was served, with dry brown bread and fruit, eaten standing to remind the community that the day's work waited, and during the day the sisters could indulge in two cups of either tea or coffee. The rest of the time thirsts were quenched with water. Brandy was kept for medicinal purposes. Sister Joan wondered if the recent shock of finding the dead tramp entitled her to a quick tot and decided that it didn't.

She bolted the kitchen door and went down the corridor into the panelled entrance hall with its sweeping staircase, the newel posts carved into a profusion of swagged oak leaves and acorns. The door leading to the parlour and the chapel with the library and storerooms above was adjacent to the kitchen wing, with the antechamber to the prioress's parlour on the left of the main entrance. Sister Joan never mounted the stairs without picturing the ladies in their long gowns and flirting their feather fans as they swept up to the great drawing-room at the head of the stairs, now divided into refectory and recreation room, with the door on the right of the gallery sealed within a wall and the cells and two bathrooms ranged over kitchen and infirmary.

Before joining her companions there was a small act of charity to perform. Sister Joan went through into the chapel wing, passing the parlour with its dividing grille where relatives and friends might visit at stated times, entering the long chapel with its simple pews for the community, its silver candlesticks and chalice, the little side altar where a statue of the Holy Virgin was poised above a vase of flowers, with a spiral staircase at the side winding to the upper storey.

She dipped her fingers in the holy water stoup, blessed herself, moved to her own accustomed seat and knelt to repeat the prayers for the dead. That much at least she could do for someone who had died alone and lain forgotten.

Her ears caught the sound of the outer door in the corridor opening and then closing. The chapel, by custom, was left open all night, so that anyone might slip in to pray or seek shelter. Only the inner door and the door at the top of the spiral staircase were firmly locked, at Detective Sergeant Mill's insistence. There had been some heated discussion about that.

'It is our custom to ensure that any passerby has the right to find spiritual help at any time of the day or night,' Mother Dorothy had said, her small frame very erect, eyes stern behind her steel-rimmed spectacles.

'Anyone who comes wandering over the moor at night isn't usually looking for spiritual help,' Detective Sergeant Mill had said grimly. 'You've some good stuff on that altar.'

'It belongs to God. If anyone were to take it God would deal with the culprit in His own way, Detective Sergeant Mill. However, since your concern for the community is, I believe, your true motive in urging this course upon us I am very willing to lock the inner door leading into the main building at the grand silence.'

The door that closed off the upper library floor had been more recently installed. Her prayers for the dead finished Sister Joan permitted herself a small, reminiscent shiver. It was odd but since the last affair[1] she had noticed that their financial worries had imperceptibly eased. Sister Katherine was fulfilling several orders for bridal gowns and first communion dresses, and Sister David had been compelled to put aside her series of books about the saints intended for children when a publisher was found in order to complete a number of translations from the Greek for which two universities were paying handsomely.

Nobody had come into the chapel. Sister Joan heard a soft footfall and then the outer door opened and closed again. She rose and went into the corridor.

It was empty, lit only by the low wattage electric light above her head. She went to the outer door and opened it, looking out into the gloom of an early summer evening. Nobody moved on the rough ground that shaded into bracken and peat. Someone coming to pray, then changing their minds and hurrying away again. She closed the door and hurried through to the main house, mounting the stairs swiftly, entering the long recreation room beyond the refectory and prostrating herself in penance for being late.

'Sisters, I pray your pardon for being late for recreation and implore Almighty God to pardon all my sins.'

'Your fault is forgiven, Sister Joan,' Mother Dorothy said briskly. 'A little lateness on this occasion was allowed you know, but you are quite an expert at stretching permission to its limit. Sister Perpetua mentioned that you had found a body.'

The expression of distaste on her face rivalled that displayed by Dame Edith Evans upon contemplation of a handbag.

'Another body,' said Sister Marie and giggled.

'Isn't it time for you and Sister Teresa to complete your kitchen duties?' Mother Dorothy enquired.

'Yes, Mother Prioress.'

[1] See *Vow of Poverty*

Both lay sisters rose with commendable speed and left the room.

'A tramp,' Sister Joan said. 'I rode Lilith a good distance since she needed a gallop and ended up over to the east. There's a chapel there – very old and broken down and unused for many years I should think. I went inside to look around and found him there. He'd been dead for a couple of days.'

'That must've been very unpleasant for you,' little Sister David said.

'I rode on to the nearest house and asked if I could use the telephone there,' Sister Joan said.

'Are there any houses out that way?' Sister Martha asked. 'It's a pretty wild area, isn't it?'

'There's a very handsome house,' Sister Joan told her. 'The housekeeper let me use the phone and gave me a cup of tea – that's an extra cup I had today, Mother Dorothy.'

'I believe the occasion justified it,' Mother Dorothy said. 'Drink water all day tomorrow to make up for it. Addiction to tea or coffee is hardly fitting for a Daughter of Compassion. Continue.'

'The police arrived,' Sister Joan said. 'Constable Petrie was in charge.'

'Not Detective Sergeant Mill?' Sister Katherine looked surprised.

'Detective Sergeant Mill is on holiday with his wife and children,' Mother Dorothy said.

Sister Joan kept careful custody of her eyes. Particular friendships, especially with married police officers, were definitely not encouraged, but it was a trifle galling that the prioress should apparently be *au fait* with Alan Mill's movements when she herself, who had assisted him on several occasions, hadn't been informed. It was an entirely forbidden and unwelcome emotion and she despised herself for it.

'The poor tramp isn't local?' Sister Mary Concepta asked in her gentle way.

'No, Sister. At least nobody there recognized him. Constable Petrie took charge most effectively and, of course, will let us know if there are any developments. He was just a drifter, I think.'

'But not unknown to God,' Mother Dorothy said. 'We shall include prayers for him in chapel tonight. I consider that quite sufficient has been said on the subject for now. I have a small piece of news of my own.'

Seven pairs of eyes looked at her expectantly.

'Brother Cuthbert returned to his community today,' Mother Dorothy said. 'He must report to his prior and spend some time with his brothers. However I gave him a letter for his superior, warmly urging that he be permitted to extend his sabbatical. I feel that his presence in the neighbourhood is of immense spiritual benefit to the whole community. I understand that Father Malone has added his own pleas.'

'I forgot about the—' Sister Joan began but was interrupted by Mother Dorothy's sharp voice.

'Sister Joan, do my eyes deceive me or are you still wearing jeans under your habit?'

'I forgot to take them off,' Sister Joan said.

'Wearing jeans when you ride Lilith is a concession to preserve your modesty,' Mother Dorothy said severely, 'but to continue to wear them in the enclosure is quite wrong, and shows a lamentably frivolous attitude to our customs, Sister. Go and change and use your discipline with particular force tomorrow evening.'

'Yes, Mother Dorothy.'

She'd mention the key that Brother Cuthbert had handed to her at a later time when she was more in favour. Meanwhile it was water all day and an extra helping of the discipline the following evening. Not, she thought gloomily, the jolliest of prospects.

'You don't really intend to join a group of hysterical women who flagellate themselves on Thursdays?' Jacob had exclaimed when she had first told him that since their separate faiths precluded marriage she had decided to join the Daughters of Compassion.

'It's more a matter of form these days,' she had argued.

'It's medieval!' Jacob's dark Semitic features had lengthened in distaste. 'Why not study Hallacah and dip yourself in the mikve like a nice little Jewish convert? It's a whole lot more civilized!'

'I wish I could,' she had answered sadly, 'but it wouldn't mean anything to me. I'd be going through the motions in order that we might get married and that's no foundation for a life together.'

'Then go and pick yourself out a Christian and marry him instead. I can't say I'll cheer you off on your honeymoon but it's a damned sight more natural!'

No, Jacob hadn't understood. She had hoped they might part friends but he had gone away with a bitter jest on his mouth and there had been no last-minute softening of his attitude. Nine years ago. Hers had been a late vocation. Nine years since she had packed away her chance of marriage and children and a career and come into the Order.

'Dreaming again, Sister Joan?' Mother Dorothy enquired. 'I said we will proceed to chapel.'

'Yes, Mother Prioress.' Sister Joan fell into line, hands clasped within the wide sleeves of her habit, eyes fixed on the floor.

'Eyes must be lowered to the ground save when engaging in necessary conversation or at recreation or in a situation which requires physical alertness such as crossing a busy road' the rule stated – that rule that was imposed on every member of the Order. Sister Joan, whose dark-blue eyes still flew upward whenever anything excited her interest, contemplated the shining, polished floor. Just ahead of her Sister Martha's black-stockinged ankles moved smoothly forward.

'Custody of the eyes is a great aid to adoration of God, allowing us to disregard all worldly affairs,' ran the rule.

Sister Martha's soles were worn and there was a small tear in the side of her shoe. She would require to have them mended soon. What on earth had made her notice Sister Martha's shoes all of a sudden? Sister Joan hastily transferred her gaze to the polished floor and waited until her mind had adjusted to holier matters.

Two hours later, kneeling for the final blessing of the day, feeling the cold drops of water sprinkle her, she was ashamed to find herself thinking of Sister Martha's shoes again.

Five in the morning was marked as it always was by the

whirring of the wooden rattle as Sister Teresa climbed the stairs and entered the dormitory wing, pausing before each door to call in her strong young voice, 'Christ is risen!'

'Thanks be to God!' Sister Joan replied, launching heself out of bed on to her knees and vainly stifling a yawn.

The morning meditation and low mass took two hours. Today it was Father Stephen, tall, handsome and certain to make bishop one day, who offered the mass, his beautiful voice creating poetry out of the ancient words, though he never stayed for a bit of a gossip over breakfast as Father Malone liked to do.

In the refectory she sipped cold water and ate the bread and the pear that comprised each portion. The day loomed ahead. Having no regular job within the community she was expected to help out where help was needed. That meant gardening, she decided. Sister Martha ran the gardens with only spasmodic help from Luther, who was simple-minded and lived over with his cousin in the Romany camp. Sister Martha would be glad of a little help.

She went downstairs and through to the kitchen to hunt out a pair of wellingtons and was caught short by the shrilling of the telephone bell.

'Yes?' She lifted the receiver. 'The Convent of the Daughters of Compassion.'

'Is that Sister Joan?' Constable Petrie's voice replied.

'Speaking.'

'We just got the forensic report, Sister. Death was due to natural causes – heart attack, so no mystery this time I'm afraid.'

'Do they know who the man was?'

'Apparently not. His pockets were empty and he'd no other identification on him.'

'Surely someone must know who he is!' Sister Joan exclaimed.

'We'll go through the missing persons file and see if we have a match,' Constable Petrie said. 'Oh, he'll be buried at public expense the day after tomorrow. I don't know if he was a Catholic or not, but Mother Dorothy might like to send a representative.'

'I'm sure she will. Thank you again, Constable Petrie.'

She replaced the receiver and went on into the kitchen, to be greeted rapturously by Alice, the young German Shepherd dog presented to the community by Detective Sergeant Mill as a potential guard dog.

'You're a good girl!' Sister Joan said, pulling on the wellingtons and going out into the yard to see to Lilith before making her way into the enclosure garden which stretched over three-quarters of an acre towards the little cemetery where past sisters slept.

Sister Martha was already at work, grubbing up weeds, and humming to herself. She broke off as Sister Joan reached her, her delicate little face brightening.

'You've come to help me, Sister Joan! That's very kind of you.'

'Where can I make myself useful?' Sister Joan enquired.

'The weeds are flourishing,' Sister Martha said. 'The recent rain encouraged them, I think. The ground elder is being particularly troublesome. It'll have to come out.'

'With Alice helping,' Sister Joan said with a grin as Alice began enthusiastically burrowing into the soft earth.

Sister Martha laughed and resumed her humming. The sound was both soothing and melodic as they worked together, long trails of ground elder being torn out and flung on to the pile.

Towards lunch-time a lanky figure shambled into view, pushing back a greasy cap perched on drooping locks and waving.

'Good morning, Luther. Have you come to help me?'

Sister Martha rose, brushing dirt off the coarse apron she wore.

'Just passing, Sister.' Luther brought his free hand from behind his back and held out an early rose. 'I got this, Sister. I pulled off the thorns.'

'That's very kind of you, Luther.' Sister Martha took the flower. 'Can you help me this afternoon? The garden's in a sad state.'

'This afternoon,' Luther repeated, lifted his cap to Sister Joan and mooched off.

'That's a lovely bloom,' Sister Joan said.

'Isn't it though!' Sister Martha contemplated it. 'I've been mounting guard over this particular rose for weeks. It's a new strain and I wasn't sure if it would take or not. Well, picking it gave Luther pleasure. I'll put it on Our Lady's altar so we can all enjoy it. Thank you for your help this morning, Sister. I'd never have managed to do so much without you.'

'You'd've done more,' Sister Joan said, heaving the last straggle of ground elder on to the pile and pulling off her gardening gloves.

Sister Martha shook her head, smiling, and went off, still humming, her neat ankles moving her away in smooth, rhythmic steps. The tear in her shoes was wider. As she hadn't worn her boots then presumably they were beyond repair.

What was it about shoes that suddenly occupied her spare thoughts? Sister Joan walked thoughtfully back to the kitchen to wash up and change out of the wellingtons. Boots. Shoes. The man in the old chapel had worn a long overcoat, its surface thick with dust. She had moved away quickly, revolted by the sickly sweet scent of encroaching decay. His shoes had been dusty too. She recalled the upturned toes with the last traces of polish on their caps. That was it! A tramp seeking shelter in an old building, lying down on a wormeaten bench and dying there of a heart attack was hardly likely to be wandering through the countryside with his shoes carefully polished.

'And it's nothing to do with me,' Sister Joan lectured herself as she went up for the mug of soup and salad sandwich and piece of fruit that lunch always consisted of.

'Sister, are you exercising Lilith this afternoon?' Mother Dorothy asked as the meal drew to a close.

'Unless I'm needed elsewhere, Mother Dorothy.'

'I think it would be a nice gesture if you were to ride over to the house from where you telephoned yesterday afternoon. Pay for the calls and tell the lady to whom you spoke what transpired, will you?'

'Oh, Constable Petrie rang earlier today,' Sister Joan remembered. 'He said that the dead man died of a heart attack and is to be buried the day after tomorrow.'

'Since you discovered the body you had better attend the funeral,' Mother Dorothy said.

'Thank you, Mother.'

The prospect of another gallop had cheered the day considerably. She went briskly to her cell to pull on the modest jeans, made a mental note to change them in time, and went down to saddle Lilith.

Mother Dorothy, appearing from a nearby doorway as was her wont, said, 'If you are offered a cup of tea or coffee, Sister, it would be very impolite to refuse it. Here is the money for the telephone calls. I'm sure it will be sufficient.'

'Thank you, Reverend Mother.'

A few minutes later she was riding through the front gates and heading across the moor. The sight of the small school building, with the old car with which Brother Cuthbert loved to tinker at the side, reminded her of the key still in her pocket. She must give it to Mother Dorothy when the opportunity arose. Meanwhile she sent a hearty good wish after Brother Cuthbert who, by now, would be back with his community in the Highlands of Scotland, and rode on, the landscape becoming wilder, rising and dipping until it sloped into the hollow of tall grasses and bracken where the old chapel stood.

It was as peaceful and deserted as it had been before the nameless tramp chose to seek shelter there and been overtaken by death. Sister Joan dismounted, tethered Lilith and went inside, treading carefully over the small piles of refuse heaped on the earth floor. The high door of the pew where the unknown man had lain was swinging open. The bench had been wiped and the surrounding floor given a cursory examination. Constable Petrie had done the expected things but hadn't used his instincts to note the polished shoes.

She scuffed her shoes musingly in the thick layer of dirt and dust convering the floor. Something white gleamed by the toe of her shoe and she bent to pick it up. It was the torn half of a piece of paper, folded up several times into a small rectangle. She unfolded it carefully, blowing off the dust as she did so, disliking the feeling of the gritty subsoil on her fingers. One side of the unfolded piece of paper was blank. On the other, a name and telephone number were scrawled.

'Michael Peter,' Sister Joan said aloud, her brow furrowing.

The telephone number was almost certainly his number too. She bit her lip, refolded the piece of paper which looked as if originally it had been torn off the lower edge of a notepad, and thrust it into her pocket.

There was no telling how long the piece of paper had been there but, apart from the surface muck, it was still pristine, the black writing on it in a bold, black hand. There was nothing to prove that the dead tramp had ever handled it, but its position so near to where he had died led her mind along an inevitable pathway. He had come in here to rest and perhaps taken the folded paper out of his pocket to check on a name or a number? Then he would have felt the intense pain in his right arm, the tightening band round his chest, the sweating and dizziness. Had he scuffed the paper with his feet as he rose in that panic of approaching death before he had laid himself painfully along the bench, telling himself he'd rise in a moment? He had never risen and the dirt had shifted and settled with each gust of wind that blew through the open door – no, that wasn't right! The pew door had been closed when she'd found the body. Would a man suffering from a fatal heart attack take the trouble to scuff a small piece of paper beneath the earth or would his instinctive action have been to thrust open the pew door in a last vain attempt to draw air into his lungs.

Whatever the answer the police had almost certainly covered the paper more completely when they entered the pew. Since it was a death due to natural causes there'd been no reason to make a thorough search of the surrounding area. Detective Sergeant Mill would have made such a close search natural causes or not, but Constable Petrie hadn't considered it necessary.

She had wasted time. That folded paper might have nothing to do with the dead man whose funeral she'd be attending the next day.

She went out, mounted up and rode across the fields with their ripening grain until the long, low house with its terraced rock garden came into view.

Today Mrs Rufus was at the door before she'd finished tethering Lilith.

'Good afternoon, Sister.' She sounded almost cheerful. 'I've just put on the kettle for a cup of tea, so you've picked the right time.'

'I must be psychic,' Sister Joan said. 'Is Lilith all right here?'

'The animal'll likely do no harm but your shoes will have to come off again,' Mrs Rufus said severely.

Sister Joan meekly removed them and followed Mrs Rufus into the kitchen.

'I'll just get another cup,' the housekeeper said. 'Did they find out who the dead body was?'

'A tramp apparently who died of a heart attack,' Sister Joan said, accepting a chair. 'Oh, Mother Dorothy gave me money for the two phone calls I made. Is it sufficient?'

'I'm sure it is. They were only local calls.' Pocketing the money Mrs Rufus asked, 'Don't you have any money of your own then?'

'We each of us get five pounds a month pocket money. Everything else goes into the general kitty,' Sister Joan explained. 'Of course, when we need new habits or shoes then Mother Dorothy – she's our prioress – gives us the money.'

'There can't be much if nobody works,' Mrs Rufus sniffed, passing the tea. 'I suppose you get dole money?'

'Afraid not!' Sister Joan grinned, drinking her tea with relish. 'The rule forbids us from taking from the State. But we can work if work's available and doesn't interfere with our religious duties. Sister David does translations from the Greek and Latin and Sister Katherine makes wedding dresses and communion frocks and Sister Martha sells our surplus fruit and vegetables in the market. I used to teach at the little school on the moor until the council closed it down and provided a bus for the children to the schools in town.'

'Dirty gyppos most of them,' Mrs Rufus said. 'If it was up to me I'd run them off.'

Sister Joan drank her tea and kept strict custody of her eyes, trying not to think about Padraic Lee who reared his two daughters and kept his caravan sparkling despite the alcoholic binges of his wife, and of simple Luther, trying to give pleasure to little Sister Martha with the offer of a forbidden rose. She wanted this woman on her side and starting a furious argument about the rights of minority groups wasn't the wisest way to go about it.

'Brother Cuthbert lodges there now,' she said mildly when she had beaten down her surge of temper. 'Perhaps you've seen him?'

'Big young chap with bright red hair and a brown sacking thing on?'

'That's Brother Cuthbert.'

'Saw him at the front of the house one day,' Mrs Rufus said. 'Standing by the wall with a mazed look on his face. He called to me something about its being a wonderfully refreshing day. I couldn't see it myself since it was pouring with rain at the time, but I figured he was either a monk or a serial killer and came in and locked all the doors. So they don't know who the dead man was? Who's going to bury him then?'

'He's to be buried tomorrow,' Sister Joan said. 'Mrs Rufus, I don't suppose you've had any tramps calling here recently?'

'Indeed I haven't!' Mrs Rufus said. 'They know better than to expect anything from here!'

'And Mr Peter wouldn't have—?'

'Mr Peter picks me up at a quarter to eight every weekday, drops me off here and goes to his shop,' Mrs Rufus said. 'He drives back around seven-thirty in the evening, gives me a lift home, and comes back here. If anyone like that had come he'd have mentioned it.'

'And Mrs Peter?' Sister Joan glanced round the shiny kitchen. 'Does she help her husband in the antique shop?'

'Her!' Mrs Rufus elevated her heavily pencilled eyebrows to an alarming level. 'That one never did a hand's turn in shop or house! Just sits around all day painting her nails and demanding eight glasses of water to keep her figure trim. Many's the time I've felt like telling her that a bit of scrubbing and polishing'd be wonderful for trimming her figure, but I know my place.'

'She's not in at the moment?'

'Went on holiday at Easter,' Mrs Rufus said.

'Yes, of course, you did tell me. She's visiting her family.'

'So Mr Peter was given to understand,' Mrs Rufus said.

'When was that?'

'Easter.'

'Two months ago? That's a long visit!'

'It can't be too long for me,' Mrs Rufus said, pouring more tea for them both. 'Mr Peter was perfectly contented until that Crystal came along. Did you ever hear such a heathen name? Crystal! He met her at a trade fair and came back married, and after that it was painted nails and pop music and endless glasses of water. I tell you straight, Sister Joan, it wouldn't bother me one bit if she never came back!'

THREE

Funerals were never cheerful affairs but this one was particularly bleak. Sister Joan laid the wreath of spring flowers at the side of the newly dug grave and turned away. Constable Petrie, in a sober black suit that smelt faintly of mothballs, came across to speak to her.

'It was good of you to come, Sister Joan,' he said, shaking hands. 'The vicar asked four of his parishioners to be volunteer pallbearers, which they kindly agreed to do, but the poor chap hasn't had much of a send-off!'

'He'll probably get a marvellous welcome on the other side,' Sister Joan said. 'You don't know yet who he was?'

'Enquiries are still proceeding,' Constable Petrie said rather grandly.

'Meaning?'

'We've circulated his description to as many police stations as possible. We couldn't very well use a photograph in the state the corpse was in. So far there's been no joy. One funny thing though! His clothes were all quite decent, and his shoes were polished. I noticed that.'

'The result of your police training, I suppose,' Sister Joan said.

'I suppose that's true. We are expected to notice things the general public misses,' Constable Petrie said modestly.

'What conclusions did you reach?' she enquired.

'That he hadn't been on the road very long,' the constable said, strolling down the path with her. 'He might've lost his memory or decided to disappear for some private reason of his

35

own. You'd be surprised how many people do that. They can't
cope with debt or they're fed up with their jobs or the wife – or
both! So they simply take off. The path. lab. estimate he was
about forty-five to fifty. Had a heart condition. He'll stay in the
files as a John Doe unless someone reports him missing.'

'And there was nothing in his pockets?'

'Not a thing,' Constable Petrie said. 'His clothes were all
chainstore bought, not particularly new but not shabby either.
No identifying marks on the body. It's a puzzle, Sister Joan.'

'It is indeed.'

The folded piece of torn paper sat guiltily at the bottom of her
pocket. She decided to say nothing about it for the moment.
There was no proof that it was even connected with the dead
man.

'I'd better be getting back to the convent,' she said.

'You didn't ride over on Lilith?'

'I drove the van down. Can I give you a lift anywhere?'

'Thank you kindly, Sister, but I'm off duty now. The wife and
I are going out to tea with her mother so I'll be getting along.'

'That'll be nice,' Sister Joan said.

'Will it?' Constable Petrie's good-humoured young face
lengthened perceptibly. 'Yes, I suppose it's nice for families to
stay in touch. You must miss that – if you have a family, that
is?'

'I've a mum and a dad and two married brothers at home,'
Sister Joan said. 'But my real family is the community now.'

'Your family don't visit?'

'They live in Manchester, so it's not really convenient. Next
year I get home leave after ten years in the Order so I'll be
going up to see them all then.'

'Nice,' said Constable Petrie without irony. 'I'll be seeing
you, Sister.'

Nice? Yes, it probably would be nice to see them all again,
Sister Joan mused, as the constable walked off briskly through
the churchyard gates. Her parents hadn't approved of her
decision to enter the religious life. For both of them the end
result of their rearing of an only daughter had been a marriage
with Joan in white on her father's arm, not Joan in white

walking alone up the aisle to be married to a Spiritual Bridegroom while her relatives watched from behind a grille.

'You know your dad absolutely adores you,' her mother said reproachfully. 'He wants you to be happy and fulfilled.'

'I will be,' Joan had said, but she doubted if her parents had ever been truly convinced.

She had left the van in the nearest car-park, feeling that it looked rather out of place at the gates of a cemetery, though the pink and white designs she'd painted over it in a burst of inspiration had been painted over, at Mother Dorothy's insistence, a 'nice respectable cream'.

She stepped out onto the pavement and walked down the long hill that led past the railway station into the town. The small steel fobwatch pinned to her belt told her that she still had time to spare before she was due back at the convent for the afternoon cup of tea and the religious discussion that preceded the private examination of one's conscience. She continued walking, turning down the narrow side street and finally admitting to herself when she arrived at the double-fronted premises of Michael Peter that she'd been aiming for the antique shop all along.

It was no wonder that she'd never gone inside the shop, she thought, pausing to look at a desk plated in ivory and gold that occupied one window, flanked in the other by a magnificent Persian vase round the base of which a brilliant red silk scarf was coiled. This was the kind of place that expert dealers frequented. Anyone hoping to pick up a bit of Victorian junk was doomed to disappointment.

She drew herself up slightly, took a deep breath, and entered the shop, somewhat more reassured when she was actually within to find that it was not so different from other antique shops after all with its glass shelves on which smaller items were tastefully ranged, its various pieces of furniture occupying odd corners, and the patina of age seemed to permeate every inch of space. Only the steep prices made the difference.

The man seated at a table at the far end of the shop with his head bent over a ledger was tall and greying with the myopic stare of someone who dislikes wearing spectacles.

Sister Joan advanced along the broad strip of carpet that ran along the floor and coughed delicately.

'Yes?'

The gentleman looked up, one finger still poised on the accounts book down which neat columns of figures marched. She thought that the old-fashioned term of 'gentleman' suited the mild, scholarly face with its high forehead and indecisive mouth. Here was a man who could quite easily be jolted out of a happy bachelor existence into matrimony with a pretty girl.

'Mr Michael Peter?'

'I am and you are – of course! you're from the convent, aren't you? If it's a charity subscription—?'

'No, I'm not collecting,' Sister Joan said, wondering why people always imagined when they saw a nun or a member of the Salvation Army that they were on the grab.

'Then how may I help you, Sister—?'

'Sister Joan. I wondered if you'd heard about the man who was found dead in the old chapel near your house.'

'I believe Mrs Rufus did mention something about it,' Michael Peter said vaguely.

'I was the one who found him.'

'How exceedingly unpleasant for you!' His expression changed to one of concern. 'Won't you sit down?'

'No, thank you. I'm really quite all right,' Sister Joan said. 'The man was buried this afternoon. His identity isn't known yet.'

'Of what did he die? Mrs Rufus mentioned heart.'

'A heart attack, yes. He was about forty-five, wearing decent clothes with no means of identification on him.'

'A drifter? There are many such these days. I don't quite see—'

'What it has to do with you? No, of course not. It's merely that I did wonder if you'd had any stranger call on you recently.'

'You mean at the house? I'm in the shop six days a week and Mrs Rufus would certainly have informed me had anyone called.'

'He might've telephoned,' Sister Joan said hopefully.

'I have an answerphone so that people can leave messages. I am not someone who enjoys telephone chats I'm afraid. No, Mrs Rufus didn't take any messages and nobody rang me up during the last couple of weeks.'

'Not your wife?' Sister Joan ventured.

A slight quiver momentarily distorted the placid features.

'Crystal dislikes the telephone,' Mr Peter said. 'She's away on holiday at the moment, visiting her sister and her parents. They went on a tour of France *en famille*.'

'A guided tour?'

'No, just the four of them in a private car. My business here made it inconvenient for me to join them.'

'When will she be home?' Sister Joan asked.

She had ventured too far. Mr Peter's eyes chilled and he gave her a long, hard stare before saying curtly, 'I fail to see how my wife's movements have anything to do with you, if you'll excuse my frankness, Sister.'

'I'm sorry,' she apologized. 'It's only that I wondered if your wife might've known the man who died, that's all.'

'Why on earth should she?' Mr Peter went on staring at her. 'Why should Crystal know a drifter who happens to die in a building not far from where we live? She's been away since Easter.'

'No, of course not.' Sister Joan gave a small, beseeching smile. 'Thank you for talking to me anyway. I wish I had the money to buy some of these things.'

'You're interested in antiques?' His expression had softened.

'I'm not very knowledgeable about them, but I do a little painting myself and so I have an interest in what's beautiful and of value.'

'I have some Klee lithographs and a rare Poussin print,' he said, thawing. 'I'll be happy to show you round any time you have an hour or two to spare. My speciality is Victorian waxworks actually. There's an extension at the back where I've set up rather an evocative exhibition. All original costumes too.'

'May I take what they call a raincheck on that?' Sister Joan asked. 'I'm due back at the convent soon.'

'And antiques require to be looked at at leisure. Of course, Sister Joan. I shall have pleasure in showing you round when it's convenient. Forgive my earlier sharpness. I'm afraid that both my wife and I are very private people.'

'I look forward to meeting her when she gets home,' Sister Joan said.

'If she can be persuaded.' He had come round the table in order to escort her politely to the door, his tall, thin figure looming over her like some Don Quixote. 'Crystal is a very shy girl, I'm afraid. She's not terribly strong so naturally I'm very pleased that she's taking this long holiday. Good afternoon, Sister.'

There was no point in hanging around. Sister Joan nodded her thanks and went out into the street. Walking to where she had parked the van she decided that the length of Mrs Peter's holiday really wasn't her business. Neither did there seem much point in turning over the piece of paper she'd found to Constable Petrie. The man had died of a heart attack. The scrawled name and telephone number might not have been connected with him at all.

The afternoon talk centred on the degree of respect accorded to the various members of the heavenly hierarchy.

'As we all know,' Mother Dorothy said, bespectacled gaze sweeping the semicircle of nuns, 'dulia or respect is paid to saints. It does not mean that we cannot study the saints from an objective, critical viewpoint but we must always bear in mind that those who are in a better position to know about these things than we are have already decided that the saints are people of heroic virtue whatever their small private faults. To Our Blessed Lady we pay hyperdulia, which is marked respect. No other human creature is worthy of that as we all know. To God alone we give adoration and worship. That is something that those who are not of the Faith find difficult to grasp. They imagine that when we kneel in front of a statue we are adoring it, when in fact we are merely using it as an aid to imagination, just as one might look at the portrait of a friend.'

'If some of the saints could come down,' Sister Gabrielle said darkly, 'they'd fly into a real temper if they saw some of the statues and portraits of them that some artists have produced.'

'Just think of St Therese of Lisieux with all those roses!' Sister Teresa exclaimed.

'Whereas the actual photographs of her show that though she was small and pretty she had a strong mouth and chin,' Mother Dorothy nodded.

'I always think that St John the Beloved must've been rather goodlooking,' Sister Mary Concepta said unexpectedly.

'While St Peter probably looked like a boxer,' Sister Perpetua supplied.

'I think we're drifting off the subject rather,' Mother Dorothy interposed. 'What we look like outside has nothing to do with our spiritual state. That is another very sound reason why we cannot possibly adore a human being since we can know only the outside of them. God can be adored because He is pure Goodness with no outer lineaments in His role as Father to distract us, and since Our Blessed Lord reflects the Father had He a human face and body we also may adore the Son without fear of falling into error. The Holy Spirit, being the love that joins the two and flows from them is coequal with both Father and Son and may also be legitimately adored. Is that clear, Sisters?'

'Do you think that the names people have reflect their inward natures?' Sister Martha enquired.

'I don't see how they can,' Sister Perpetua said. 'Parents can't possibly tell what the baby's going to turn out like.'

'Perhaps their subconscious guides them,' Sister Katherine offered.

'There was a boy called Samson at our school. He was the biggest coward you could ever meet,' Sister Teresa said.

Mother Dorothy's gavel rapped sharply.

'To adore is to regard with uncritical and total worship,' Sister Gabrielle said.

'Doesn't it ever seem odd to you that we regard with total and uncritical worship a Creator of whom by His very nature we can know nothing for certain?' Sister Joan said.

'You forget that we have Our Blessed Lord,' Mother Dorothy said.

' "No man comes to the Father but through me",' Sister David quoted.

'Exactly, Sister. We simply cannot apply human criteria to these problems. Now, as time is getting on I suggest we leave the discussion there and go to our private examination of concience with time to reflect on our faults. Sister Joan, you went to the funeral of that poor man?'

'Yes, Mother Dorothy. They haven't found out who he was yet though.'

'Very sad for his family if he has any, but his name will certainly be known in Heaven. Thank you for going. *Dominus vobiscum.*'

'*Et cum spiritu sancto,*' the community chorused, the younger sisters kneeling briefly, the older and more rheumaticky ones taking rather longer about it.

The day moved tranquilly to its close. Sister Joan filled in her spiritual diary, and was faintly astonished to discover that she'd managed to cut down her faults by three during the past week. Not that it made much difference, she reflected, since she usually got rid of one fault only to have another pop up in its place!

Seated on the floor of her cell, her legs tucked beneath her in the customary fashion, she reached for her sketchbook and began idly to draw, her mind still running on the topics discussed earlier. The members of the Order either kept their own names if they were suitable or chose others when they entered the religious life. Her name was her given one. Sister Perpetua had mentioned once that she had chosen her name because of the legend of that martyr who had combed her long hair before going into the arena to be killed by the lions. Sister Joan's pencil etched a hefty Perpetua, dragging a comb through greying ginger hair while a very small lion cowered before her. Mother Dorothy followed, waving a bunch of flowers, with Sister Martha sweeping up the leaves on her heels. Sister Joan's lips curved into amusement as her pencil flew over the paper.

Other sketches took shape. A tall, thin Don Quixote with a blonde bimbo on his arm, a woman composed of balls and lengths of twine scowling at her pony – the bell rang, signalling that only half an hour remained before supper. Sister Joan shoved her book on the shelf, rose with the nimbleness of long habit and went down to help Sister Marie with the laying of the tables.

At recreation she pleased Sister Mary Concepta by playing Scrabble with her, though it was more effort than entertainment since with the advancing years Sister Mary Concepta's grasp of spelling, never very strong, had deteriorated markedly, a fact she was unable to admit. She merely remarked placidly that spelling had changed since her young days and carefully jotted down the extra ten points she'd just won.

At the back of her thoughts lay the unknown man in his anonymous grave, the young wife touring France with her family and not contacting her husband, the torn strip of paper folded in the bottom of her pocket, the key—

'Sisters, would you please excuse me for a few moments?' she said hurriedly. 'I forgot to tell Mother Dorothy something!'

'It only wants twenty minutes to chapel,' Sister David observed.

'Would you like me to check on the holy water and the candles for you, Sister?'

Sister David, who combined her duties of librarian and secretary and her own translation work with the post of sacristan looked pleased, since her recreation was always cut short by the necessity for her to get the chapel ready.

'If it isn't a great trouble to you, Sister—?' she said, pushing up her spectacles on her snub nose and favouring Sister Joan with one of her unexpectedly sweet smiles.

'No trouble,' Sister Joan said, relinquishing her place at the Scrabble board to Sister Marie who couldn't spell either and making a graceful exit, only slightly marred by the sound of Sister Perpetua's voice echoing after her, 'That child is so restless! Give her half a chance and she'd rush off to raise the siege of Orleans all over again!'

'I thought it was Bosnia that was under siege,' Sister Mary Concepta said, puzzled.

Sister Joan choked back a giggle and went down the stairs and across the hall to the wide antechamber beyond which the prioress had her parlour. Mother Dorothy usually joined them for only part of the recreation, choosing to use the free time to catch up with her own work, generally the adding up and painful balancing of the monies on which the convent supported itself.

Sister Joan's tap on the door elicited a brisk invitation to enter. Doing so, kneeling for the customary ritual greeting, she was struck as she always was by the contrast between the opulent panelling on the walls and the gilding on the cornices of what had once been a gracious drawing-room and the small, trim, purple-habited figure of the prioress. Purple was worn during the five-year-term of office. After that the erstwhile head of the community returned to the light-grey habit with the addition of a narrow purple band on the sleeve to remind her of her previous status.

'We seem to be holding our own financially so far this year,' Mother Dorothy said, putting down her pen, 'but there's very little security these days! If we have the hot summer the experts are predicting that won't help the harvest, so we must bear that in mind. What can I do for you, Sister?'

'Brother Cuthbert gave me the key of the schoolhouse for you, Mother Prioress, and I forgot all about it,' Sister Joan said.

'Thank you, Sister.' Mother Dorothy looked musingly at the key. 'It will seem odd now that Brother Cuthbert isn't there. Happily I've every expectation of his coming back in about a month. Meanwhile we have an empty property on our hands.'

'Perhaps we could rent it out for a few weeks?' Sister Joan suggested.

Mother Dorothy gave one of her rare chuckles.

'The last time we left it to you to find temporary lodgers,' she said dryly, 'the results were – somewhat unfortunate!'[1]

'I only thought—'

'Actually it isn't a bad idea,' Mother Dorothy said. 'There may be a birdwatcher who requires somewhere cheap and quiet. Sister, I'll leave the key with you. Don't rush about trying to find someone, but if the Lord provides a temporary lodger

[1] See *Vow of Fidelity*

then I leave it to your good judgement. You had better go over there tomorrow with cleaning material and fresh bedding. When you want something to happen it's always as well to give the Lord a little nudge by behaving as if what is desired was already settled.'

'Like thanking God for something before the prayer is granted.'

'Ah, St Paul was a sound psychologist in so many ways,' the prioress said. 'It's a pity that he has fallen out of fashion in some quarters. Mind you, the mind boggles to imagine his reaction to the notion of female priests.'

'We may well get there eventually,' Sister Joan ventured.

'Not in my lifetime,' Mother Dorothy said firmly. 'Adam was created first and we push ourselves forward at our peril. Men do not respect domineering women.'

'No, Mother Prioress,' Sister Joan said meekly, longing to remark that Father Malone lived in such great respect of the prioress that he hardly took a step without seeking her approval.

'That will be all, Sister.'

'Thank you, Mother Dorothy. Oh, I offered to get the chapel ready for service. Have I your permission?'

'Of course. Sister David seldom gets a break. *Dominus vobiscum.*'

'*Et cum spiritu sancto.*'

Sister Joan knelt, put the key back in her capacious pocket and went out across the hall to the chapel wing.

Darkness had almost fallen and only the red sanctuary lamp glowed at the side of the altar. Sister Joan went down the side aisle and up the three steps to light the white candles at each side of the veiled Host. Lighting candles was, she thought, one of the more pleasant tasks in the convent. As each flame sprang into life she felt a small, corresponding glow within herself.

At the side of the altar a shadow flitted silently away. She swung round with a stifled exclamation, in time to see the door into the outer passage open and close. Quick footsteps sounded and the outside door opened and closed with a decided thump.

'To interrupt the preparation of the chapel save for the most urgent reasons is to disturb the rhythmic tranquillity one is trying to create.'

Why did she have to remember Mother Dorothy's sayings at the most inconvenient moment? She lit the last candle, knelt, replaced the taper, went into the tiny sacristy where the priest, when he came, robed himself, checked on the holy water for the asperges and, still congratulating herself on her lack of curiosity, knelt swiftly and made for the outer door.

The rough ground that shaded into open moorland was dark, with the occasional dazzle of the rising moon as it drifted through the sable clouds to mitigate the gloom. It would've been useless to follow since she had no torch with her and, in any case, the chapel was open for anyone who cared to come. Perhaps it had been Luther who came now and then to gaze adoringly at the statue of the Holy Virgin on her side altar.

'She looks just like my mam when she were young,' he had said once earnestly.

No, not Luther. Luther would've greeted and offered to help. They had been a woman's footsteps anyway.

Sister Joan came back into the chapel, her eye caught by a gleam of white near the altar. She went over and bent to pick it up, her fingers touching the fine lawn of a lace-edged handkerchief, the sort of handkerchief that never knows the indignity of having a nose blown into it. Smoothing it out, moving closer to the lighted candles, she traced the initial C in black silk embroidered with a flourish across one corner. C for Crystal? In that case what was it doing here?

FOUR

The van bumped gently over the tussocks of grass and came to rest at the side of the old schoolhouse. Sister Joan opened the door and allowed Alice, sitting alertly at her side, to bound out, barking joyfully. If there was anything Alice enjoyed more than a run it was a ride in a vehicle – any vehicle! She was growing into a fine dog, her coat glossy, her nature sweet – too sweet for a guard dog, Sister Joan considered, hauling out her cleaning materials. Instead of raising the alarm when strangers approached Alice greeted them with wagging tail and begged for titbits.

'If we had any money,' Sister Gabrielle had pronounced gloomily, 'that dog would lead the burglar to the safe and bark out the combination!'

Sister Joan took out the key and opened the door, feeling as usual a sharp nostalgia that overcame her whenever she entered here. The sturdily constructed stone building which had once been part of the Tarquin estate and had passed into the ownership of the community when the property was sold to the Order had been used as a school for local children who couldn't get down into town to the state schools. Her first task at the Cornwall House had been to teach there. It hadn't been an easy job, she recalled, and there had been incidents connected with this building that had challenged her courage, but she had felt affection for the children, some from the Romany camp, others the children of local farmers, and she had relished the sense of independence the work had given her. Now a school bus collected the children and bore them down into town every morning and disgorged them at various collecting points at teatime.

'Our main function is to adore God constantly through prayer, meditation, and deeds of charity,' Mother Dorothy was fond of saying. 'Everything in our lives must centre upon that.'

Perhaps it was for the best that the school had closed down, thus confining her more within the convent, but she missed the bright faces, the elaborate excuses that the smarter pupils had concocted to explain away work left undone, the pleasure of being alone when the children had gone home and she sat at her desk for a few minutes to relish the peace and quiet.

'Not much adoring there, girl!' she admonished herself, stepping into the short passage that separated the cloakroom and two toilets from the large classroom.

Since Brother Cuthbert had arrived the cloakroom with its row of empty pegs had served him as a washroom while in the larger room he had slept on a camp bed, cooked his two meals a day on a tabletop cooker and filled the cupboard with the books he borrowed from the convent library. Some of them were still here. It was a hopeful sign that he intended to return. She ran her eye along the titles, smiling. Brother Cuthbert had no liking for theological works, preferring to derive his spiritual nourishment from the church and the moors. Instead he favoured thrillers and love stories that ended happily with everybody reconciled and a pretty wedding.

Outside Alice barked on the high, excited note that heralded a friend – which meant absolutely nothing since to Alice anything on two legs was a friend!

Sister Joan went out to the front and looked round. The dog was begging coyly, head on one side, eyes pleading, though the figure shrinking against the side of the van didn't seem to be applauding the trick.

'Alice, down! Down, girl!' Sister Joan went forward, reaching to grasp Alice's collar. 'She won't hurt you. There's no need to be scared.'

The young woman had straightened up slightly, pulling her coat about her slim frame, a slight smile quivering on her unpainted mouth. Her dark hair was pulled to the back of her head in a ponytail and her eyes, a soft hazel brown, lifted to scan Sister Joan's face with a mixture of apprehension and curiosity.

'I wasn't doing any harm,' she said defensively.

'I'm sure you weren't,' Sister Joan said heartily.

'You're Sister Joan from the convent, aren't you?' the stranger said.

'Yes, I am. How did you know?'

'I read something about you in the newspaper,' the other said. 'It said that you solved crimes.'

'Oh Lord!' Sister Joan grimaced.

Publicity was the one thing she had always eschewed, being in complete agreement with her prioress on that matter.

'Helping the police with their enquiries is the duty of a good citizen,' Mother Dorothy had lectured, 'but personal publicity is highly undesirable. We are not in the religious life to gain notoriety in the outside world.'

'That article,' she said now, 'was grossly exaggerated. However my photograph didn't appear in it so how—?'

'I was walking past the convent grounds,' the young woman said. 'There were two nuns working there. One of them called to Sister Joan, and I had a glimpse of you as I came to a low part of the wall.'

'Were you in the chapel last night?' Sister Joan asked.

'And a couple of evenings ago.' The other blinked nervously, hands still clutching her brown coat. 'I wanted to speak to you but I funked it.'

'Look, why don't you come into the schoolhouse and I'll make us both a cup of tea?' Sister Joan suggested. 'You look as if you could do with one.'

'I could do with a bit of a wash,' the other said. 'I slept in that old car last night.' She nodded towards the broken-down vehicle in the depths of which Brother Cuthbert loved to fiddle.

'Come inside,' Sister Joan said promptly.

The stranger looked as if she couldn't endure much more stress. Noting the pallor of her skin, the dark shadows under her eyes, Sister Joan decided that practical help was required.

'There's no hot water but I can boil up a kettle and then,

while you're washing, I'll put it on again for a cup of tea,' she said. 'Brother Cuthbert left tea and sugar behind, but there's no milk, I'm afraid. However I'll see if I can rustle up a biscuit.'

'Is Brother Cuthbert the teacher?' the young woman enquired, following her indoors, with Alice, ears pricked at the idea of a biscuit, bringing up the rear.

'No, this hasn't been a school for ages,' Sister Joan said. 'Brother Cuthbert is a monk who lives here now as a kind of semi-hermit. He's away at present, staying with his community up in the Highlands. I'll get the kettle on.'

Leaving the young woman to make her toilet she took the boiling water into the cloakroom, poured it into the tall jug there, called cheerfully to the locked door of the lavatory that the water was ready, and went back into the larger room to make the tea and lay out the half packet of digestive biscuits and the apple she unearthed in the cupboard.

'I feel better now.'

The young woman had come in, her brown coat over her arm. Her face had a touch of colour now and her hair had been tidied but the brown skirt and sweater she wore did nothing to flatter her colouring.

'Have some tea and biscuits,' Sister Joan said, indicating a chair. 'Now, suppose we start at the beginning. Is this your handkerchief?'

She fluttered the lace-edged piece of lawn with its boldly embroidered initial.

'Yes.' The other folded her hands round the mug of hot, milkless tea. 'I left it in the chapel. I hoped that you might find it and come to find me. I couldn't have talked to you in the church. Someone might've come in and seen me.'

'Is your name Crystal?' Sister Joan asked.

'Caroline.' The other drew in her breath sharply. 'Why did you say Crystal? Do you know her?'

'I've heard of her. You're Caroline who?'

'Hayes. Caroline Hayes.' The young woman drank her tea shiveringly. 'Crystal's my younger sister.'

'You're on tour in France!'

'France?' The other looked puzzled. 'I've never been to

France. What's this about touring France?'

'At Easter Crystal went to France with her family,' Sister Joan said.

'That's what Michael Peter told you?'

'Mrs Rufus actually.'

'She's the housekeeper, isn't she?'

'You've not met her?'

Caroline shook her head. 'This is the first time I've been down into Cornwall,' she said. 'We weren't invited to the wedding.'

'Your sister's wedding to Michael Peter?'

Caroline nodded again. 'There's only a year between Crystal and me,' she said. 'She's twenty-two. When we were children people used to remark on how pretty she was and then they'd look at me and say, "Oh, that one's sure to be clever"! And I'm not! I did a course of shorthand and typing and I do temporary work, but I'm not clever.'

'Is Crystal clever?'

'I don't know.' Caroline drank more tea, put down the mug, and frowned. 'She's only pretty, I think. She's very amusing and she sits with a rapt, listening look on her face when other people are talking but half the time I doubt if she's following what they're saying. She's probably trying to decide whether to wear pink or coral lipstick, or if she ought to shorten her skirt or something. She's very sweet but a bit naive.'

'She met Michael Peter at a trade fair?'

'Last year,' Caroline nodded. 'She used to get jobs as a receptionist at business conferences and that kind of thing. She was very decorative and the clients liked her.'

'She didn't live at home?'

'No, she had a room somewhere in London.' A dull red stained Caroline's pale cheeks. 'To be honest I think that now and then she worked for an – an escort agency and – well, she never would say exactly where she was living. It used to worry Dad terribly, but after Mum died he began to recognize that he couldn't go on protecting her all her life and—'

'Your mother's dead?'

'Two years ago,' Caroline said. 'That's partly why I went on living at home. Dad isn't too well at the moment and he really needs someone to keep an eye on him.'

'So you lived at home and Crystal didn't?'

'She visited us quite often,' Caroline said quickly. 'She used to bring little presents for us. She was always good at choosing presents for people. A bottle of cologne, this handkerchief, that kind of thing. She really is a nice person.'

'But she didn't ask you to the wedding?'

'It was a very quiet one,' Caroline said excusingly. 'Dad was having a long spell of tests in hospital and I was trying to decide whether or not it'd be a good idea to sell our flat. It's on the fourth floor and the lift doesn't even work, and we hadn't seen Crystal for several weeks. Then she rang up out of the blue and said she was married and living in Cornwall!'

'You didn't think of coming down to visit her?'

'I didn't want to push myself. Crystal liked her privacy. We all like that, don't we? I rang her once but there was an answerphone on and I put the receiver down. I can never think what to say to a machine. I wrote to her though and Dad and I got a nice number of letters back, telling us that she had a beautiful home and that her husband absolutely adored her. We rather hoped she'd come over at Christmas but she sent a hamper of exotic fruits and a side of smoked salmon instead. Oh, and cards signed by both of them. I wrote back but there wasn't very much to say. After Dad got out of hospital we were busy arranging for the sale of the flat and he has to go into hospital for a week now and then for treatment.'

'Miss Hayes—'

'Caroline, please.'

'Caroline, why are you here? Why did you want to see me?'

'We haven't had a letter from Crystal for over two months,' Caroline said.

'Didn't you telephone?'

'Dad did – twice. He rang up and Michael Peter, Crystal's husband, picked up the phone and said that Crystal was away visiting a friend but she'd get in touch when she returned. The second time Dad just got the answerphone and though he left a message nobody rang back. Since he had to go into hospital last week I decided to come into Cornwall and find out what was going on.'

'You went to the house.'

'No – no, I meant to go but I lost my nerve.' Caroline flushed dully again.

'Why? Surely it've been the natural thing to call and ask if your sister was there?'

'I went to the local police,' Caroline said.

'Before going to the house? That's a bit drastic!'

'Not really.' Caroline hesitated, then fumbled in the pocket of her brown coat which she had hung over the back of her chair. 'I said that Crystal hasn't written or phoned since Easter but she sent me this.'

Withdrawing her hand from the coat pocket she opened her palm to show the letter C fashioned in gold and depending from a small loop.

'A present?' Sister Joan asked.

'No. We each of us had one. Dad bought them for us. Hers was gold and mine's silver.' Caroline drew it out on the end of its chain from beneath the neck of her sweater.

'Your sister sent you hers?'

'In a little package. We had an agreement – one of those arrangements you make in fun, never expecting that anything will come of it. It was a joke really. If you're ever in deadly danger send me your initial – you know the sort of thing. But even though we were laughing we meant it deep down.'

'When did you receive this?'

'That's the awful thing,' Caroline said, catching her breath on a little sob. 'She posted it just after Easter but she didn't send it to the flat. Perhaps she was worried about Dad seeing it and panicking or something, or perhaps she was not thinking straight herelf. She sent it to the agency where I get temporary work from time to time but they moved premises and the new people didn't bother to send mail on for ages so I only got it last week.'

'And you went to the police?'

'First I had to get Dad into hospital,' Caroline said. 'I told him that I might take a few days off and not to worry if I didn't pop in and see him while he was there, and then I came here. I did go up to the house. It was after dark and Michael Peter was just coming back from somewhere in his car. I guessed it was him from the description Crystal gave us.'

'He'd probably just run Mrs Rufus home.'

'The housekeeper? Yes, Crystal mentioned her in one of her letters. Anyway I stood in the shadows and watched him get out of the car. The headlights were still on. He went up the path and opened the front door and switched on a light and then he came back to switch off the headlights and lock the door. He was grinning.'

'Grinning?'

'Yes. Not smiling but stretching his mouth. I could see his teeth. I never saw anybody look like that before. It was – anyway I stood where I was and he turned and went up to the house again. I stayed in a local bed and breakfast and the next morning I went to the police.'

'What did they say?' Sister Joan asked.

'I spoke to a detective sergeant. Mill. Tall, dark, rather good-looking.'

'I know him.'

'He was very polite but he didn't take me very seriously,' Caroline said. 'He said that people could sometimes go for ages without contacting their relatives and that unless there was some reason to fear for Crystal's safety I'd nothing to go on.'

'Did you show him the initial that your sister had sent?'

'I was going to,' Caroline said, 'but he sounded so sensible, so down to earth, that I felt a bit silly about saying anything. Anyway he advised me to call at the house and ask where Crystal was and to go back to him if anything struck me as suspicious.'

'Did you go to the house?' Sister Joan asked.

'I hung around for a bit. I kept out of sight but I'm sure Crystal wasn't at home. There was a middle-aged woman there, brushing the steps and raking the gravel for a bit, and I saw her passing the windows inside the house later on, but there was no sign of Crystal. It was a nice day and she'd have come out to sit in the garden or take a walk or something surely. She loves flowers.'

'I can't understand why you didn't just ring the front doorbell and ask.'

'Because I don't want to put him on his guard,' Caroline said tensely. 'If I'd started asking questions of the housekeeper she might've mentioned it to him when he came home and then he'd know someone was looking for Crystal. He'd be on his guard, don't you see?'

'So you came looking for me?'

'I didn't know what to do,' Caroline said. 'I went to the local cinema and sat there, trying to work out some course of action. There was a film on – a Whoopi Goldberg film about nuns. Have you seen it?'

'We don't go to the cinema.'

'It was a comedy. Anyway I suddenly remembered that article I'd read and I came out and asked someone if the Order of the Daughters of Compassion had a convent anywhere near. They told me it was on the moors, so I walked there.'

'It's five miles.'

'I know. I don't drive myself and there didn't seem to be a bus. Anyway I went in the hopes of seeing you but it was dusk when I got there. I said a prayer in your chapel and came away.'

'And came back twice? You must be a good walker.'

'I got a lift in from a man driving a van. He had gold hoops in his ears and smelt rather strongly of fish.'

'That was probably Padraic Lee,' Sister Joan said. 'He does rather a lot of fishing.'

'You were in the convent garden but the other nun was with you,' Caroline said. 'I went away again, and then last evening I made up my mind to take the plunge and pluck up the courage to speak to you but when the moment came – you must think me an awful fool!'

'You slept in the old car last night?'

'I was so tired,' Caroline said. 'I'd walked here and when it didn't work out, when I turned tail again, it was dark and my legs ached and I'd noticed the building when I passed it before so I decided to stay overnight if I could, but the door was locked so I slept in the old car. I hope it wasn't trespassing!'

'I shouldn't think so,' Sister Joan said.

'Anyway I've seen you now,' Caroline said. 'I'm sorry to have taken up your time. I've been listening to myself rattling on and it all sounds quite impossible, doesn't it? The police won't do anything and it was—'

'They can't,' Sister Joan said. 'Nobody's been reported missing. Yes, I know that you tried but you didn't have much to go on. You really should have gone to the house and made preliminary enquiries there.'

'I thought of that but after I saw Michael Peter's face – that fixed grin – in the headlights of his car I just couldn't,' Caroline said. 'Sister, I really hoped that you might undertake to do some enquiring on my behalf. I can pay.'

'I'm not a private detective,' Sister Joan said in alarm. 'It just happens that I've been able to help the police in their investigations now and then, but I'm a nun. I don't go round picking up clues and interviewing suspects.'

'It was rude of me to bother you,' Caroline said, reaching for her coat and pulling it on. 'I'm sorry.'

'What will you do now?'

'I don't know.' Caroline gave a sad little shrug. 'Dad comes out of hospital in a week and he'll certainly start worrying if we don't hear from Crystal soon. I can't stay on in the town. Michael Peter has an antique shop there and I could easily run into him. Crystal took some family photographs with her when she left home and she's got a very clear one of me which he might recognize if he met me. The truth is that I don't know what to do!'

'You could stay here,' Sister Joan said impulsively.

'Here?' Caroline looked round.

'Brother Cuthbert won't be back for at least a month,' Sister Joan said. 'We were hoping to rent it out cheaply for a few weeks to a birdwatcher or someone. Nobody would disturb you. In fact most people wouldn't even realize you were here.'

'I'm not sure.' Caroline bit her lip and gazed beseechingly.

'And if you're worried about supplies I can pick them up for you in town when I do the convent shopping. Where are your things?'

'I only brought a small bag with me,' Caroline said. 'It's at the bed and breakfast place.'

'Which is—?'

'In Station Road. I booked in there because it wasn't near the centre of town.'

'Then why don't we drive down there in the van? You can pick up your bag, pay the bill and I'll drive you back again. Look, nobody's going to notice you particularly. This may be a small town but there are always tourists coming and going, and anyway the housekeeper told me that Michael Peter spends all day in his shop when he's not off on a buying trip.'

'You've been asking questions about him already?' The other looked at her in bewilderment.

'Nothing to do with your visit,' Sister Joan said, hoping that was true. 'What do you think about my offer? Mother Dorothy, our prioress, has left it to me to rent out if I can. Say, twenty-five pounds a week? The amenities are a bit primitive.'

'That's very cheap! Thank you.'

'Let's get in the van then. Don't mind Alice. She's very friendly and she loves going for a drive.'

Caroline scurried to the van and sat throughout the three-mile journey into town with her hand carefully shielding her face, emerging at the bed and breakfast establishment to hurry up the steps, emerging five minutes later with a suitcase which she put in the back of the van before taking her place in the passenger seat.

'I have a few groceries to get,' Sister Joan said. 'I'll park the van in the station car-park and leave you with Alice. Just give me fifteen minutes.'

'Can you get some for me too?' Caroline pressed some notes into her hand. 'Just the basics. I don't eat very much at the best of times and right now I just feel so anxious!'

'Coffee, sugar, powdered milk, bread, butter, some fruit, eggs, a packet of kippers, some tins of beans? Right then! Stay here, Alice.'

Driving the van into the car-park out of which a covered underpass reached to the station she alighted, gave Caroline a reassuring smile, and strode off towards the nearest supermarket.

She went briskly round, paid for her purchases, loaded them into the two large string bags she carried, and started back towards the van.

'Good day, Sister!'

She swung round, the bags bumping against her legs, and stared wordlessly up into the lean face of Michael Peter.

'I'm on my way to catch a train,' he said. 'It's more pleasant to use public transport in London, don't you think? May I help you with your shopping?'

'No, thank you.' She recovered her wits with an effort. 'Are you going on business?'

'There's an auction at a mews cottage in Chelsea. I thought it might be worth a look. Oh, you'll be pleased to hear that I had a telephone call from my wife last night.'

'Oh,' Sister Joan said blankly.

'Yes indeed.' He showed improbably white teeth in a stretched smile. 'They are on the move, staying at *pensions* and *auberges* as far as I can gather. The line wasn't very good. She has asked for a couple of extra weeks which I agreed to, of course.'

'Yes, of course.'

'Well, I'd better get on. I don't want to miss my train.'

He raised his hat in a courtly, old-fashioned manner and walked off, carrying with apparent ease his large suitcase.

'I was getting worried,' Caroline said, watching her face above the lever of the van window as Sister Joan arrived.

'I think I got all the groceries,' Sister Joan said.

There was no point in alarming the young woman by mentioning her meeting with Michael Peter.

Driving back again she asked casually, 'Will your father expect you to telephone him?'

'He thinks I'm with my friends, so he won't expect to hear anything until I get back. That's why I want to find something out fairly quickly if I can. They'll finish the present series of tests in about a week and I really don't like to leave him to cope alone. Since Mum died he's been rather more dependent on me than he cares to admit.'

'Which hospital is he in?' She swung the van on to the

moorland track.

'It's a private hospital – the Florence Nightingale Heart Foundation in Richmond,' Caroline said. 'It's rather expensive but they get wonderful care. Shall I pay you the twenty-five pounds in advance?'

'That'll sweeten Mother Dorothy. Look, I can't stay to help you settle in, but I'll be over first thing in the morning. The electricity isn't connected but there are oil lamps. Can you manage them?'

'I'm sure I can. You're being very kind.'

'Well, here's the key then. Can you manage your bag and the groceries? Try to rest and not fret too much. God bless!'

Her cheerful expression faded slightly as, having helped Caroline to alight, she waved her hand and drove on. According to Michael Peter his wife was touring France with her sister, her father and a dead mother, and had telephoned him the previous evening.

According to Caroline Hayes her sister hadn't been in touch since Easter and had sent at about that time the secret call for help agreed between the sisters.

'May I make a telephone call, Mother Prioress?'

Having deposited the groceries in the kitchen and scolded Alice for wetting in the back of the van she accosted Mother Dorothy as the latter emerged from her parlour.

'A very quick one,' Mother Dorothy said. 'The lecture begins in five minutes.'

'Thank you, Mother. Oh, I have a short-term tenant for the schoolhouse. A young woman called Caroline Hayes. She's anxious for a few days' peace and quiet and she's paid twenty-five pounds.'

'That was very quick, Sister! Is she a respectable young woman?'

'A shorthand typist from London.'

'Seeking the peace that we in the religious life take for granted. Thank you, Sister.'

Mother Dorothy crossed towards the chapel wing, leaving Sister Joan free to dart into the kitchen corridor where the telephone was positioned on the wall.

'The Florence Nightingale Heart Foundation.' Having obtained the number from the operator she rang it and was answered by an official-sounding voice which assured her she was connected to the hospital.

'I'm enquiring about a Mr Hayes. He's undergoing tests or treatment at present?'

'Further treatment for an enlarged heart yes, but he didn't turn up for his appointment,' the voice informed her. 'Apparently family business took him down to Cornwall.'

'Oh dear, I hadn't heard—'

'We were rather anxious about his cancellation,' the voice confided. 'His health does give cause for concern. If you ring again in a few days—'

'Thank you.'

Sister Joan replaced the receiver, thinking of the middle-aged tramp with the shiny shoes who had died of a heart attack in the old chapel. It began to look as if father as well as sister had become anxious about Crystal Peter's welfare and come into Cornwall to make enquiries. The problem was whether or not to tell Constable Petrie or to wait until Alan Mill returned.

FIVE

'Are you going into town this morning, Sister?'

Sister Gabrielle came into the kitchen where Sister Joan was helping Sister Marie to scrub some ancient pans.

'Yes, Sister. We have a short-term tenant for the old schoolhouse while Brother Cuthbert is away and I'm going down to check that she's settled in comfortably.'

'I need some aspirin. Sister Perpetua forgot to ask you for it when you last went down into town shopping. Would it be a bother?'

'No bother,' Sister Joan said cheerfully.

She was in a buoyant mood this morning, having made her decision, slept well, and spent a couple of hours helping out with the more basic work in the kitchen.

'You go now, Sister. I can finish off the rest,' Sister Marie said helpfully.

Sister Joan rinsed her hands, received several other small commissions from some of the other sisters, and went out to the van, leaving Alice to whine after her in Sister Marie's grasp.

The little schoolhouse seemed deserted. For a moment she wondered if Caroline had lost her nerve again and stolen away in the night but, as she climbed down from the van, the door opened and the young woman appeared on the threshold, her lank hair neatly plaited at each side of her thin face, the unremarkable sweater and skirt carefully brushed.

'Good morning, Sister. I slept very soundly,' she greeted her.

'So did I. I brought some extra blankets for you. It can get chilly at night and Brother Cuthbert doesn't feel the cold. I'm going on into town so if there's anything you need I can drop it off on my way back. Mother Dorothy was very pleased that we'd found a temporary tenant by the way.'

'You're being very kind.' Caroline took the two thick blankets and went indoors.

Sister Joan's cheerful mood darkened a little. Not so kind, she reflected, when so far she had given no hint to the other that the father she believed to be in hospital had been buried in an unmarked grave. When she'd talked to Constable Petrie she would probably have the unpleasant duty of breaking the news to her.

'I just brewed a cup of tea. Have you time for one?'

'Not for me,' Sister Joan said, 'but I'll watch you drink it if you like. Have you made up your mind exactly what you plan to do?'

'Not really.' Caroline frowned, biting her lip. 'I can take walks near the house, I suppose, while Michael Peter's at work. I honestly don't know, Sister. I just have this feeling that I ought to be on the spot for a bit.'

'In case your sister comes back?'

'Oh, I wish she could just knock at the door right this minute and send all my fears flying!' Caroline said with sudden intensity. 'She has a habit of popping in when she isn't expected. Dad used to say she was like a will o' the wisp, but since she got married he doesn't talk about her so often. I think he was hurt not to be invited to the wedding or asked to meet her husband.'

'You sound like a very close family,' Sister Joan said.

'Yes.' Caroline spoke softly, her face wistful. 'We sort of stuck together you know. London isn't a very neighbourly place and Mum was rather a shy person. She found it hard to make friends there.'

'You're not from London originally?'

'No, we were born in Marsden Close. It's a little village in Nottinghamshire, just a road and a post office and a general store, three churches and six pubs!' Caroline said. 'We lived there until we were almost ready to transfer to the senior school. Then Dad decided that it might be more profitable to move to the City. He was a bank clerk then but after Mum died we found out his heart condition was much worse than we'd imagined and he took early retirement with a disability pension. I have to find out what's been going on within the next week or so. He'll be frantic if he comes out of hospital and finds that I'm gone still.'

'I'll make a few discreet enquiries while I'm in town,' Sister Joan promised. 'But I can't do very much. Look, if you're nervous about going up to the house to ask about Crystal I might be able to get leave to go with you.'

'Maybe I'll do that,' Caroline said hesitatingly. 'Oh, if it was me gone Crystal just wouldn't take a second thought. She'd march up there and camp on Michael Peter's doorstep until she got a straight answer. She's younger than I am but she has tons more courage. Dad says that she's a typical Aries and I'm a typical Pisces – one all energy and the other all mush!'

'I'm sure you'll find that she's all right,' Sister Joan said. 'She might've sent the initial as a joke?'

'It wasn't a joking matter,' Caroline said. 'Anyway there's the letter.'

'What letter?'

'I told you she wrote quite often after she was married. She kept saying that as soon as business was easier she and Michael would come up and see us. Then she sent us a brief letter just before Easter. Fortunately I take the post and I read it before Dad got up before breakfast and decided to keep it to myself until we heard from her again, but we never did.'

'May I see the letter?'

'You can keep it.' Caroline went over to her suitcase and opened it, bringing out the envelope. 'I don't know if it'll help you.'

'I'll read it later.' Sister Joan put it in her pocket and stood up. 'I'd better get down into town. Anything you need?'

'No. I'll be fine. Thank you, Sister.'

She stood up, politely showing her visitor to the door. By the time Sister Joan was behind the wheel again the door of the little building had firmly closed.

Sister Joan parked the van in the station yard and walked

back down the main street. Her first call had to be at the police station.

A young constable was behind the reception desk when she walked in. Young and unfamiliar, she summed up, her mouth curving with amusement as she saw how hastily he shoved a girlie magazine under a pile of documents and straightened up as he saw her walk in.

'Good morning. Is Constable Petrie around?' she asked.

'I'm afraid not, Sister—?'

'Sister Joan. Is he on duty today?'

'He's off sick, Sister. I was drafted in from Penzance to keep the shop open so to speak.'

'Sick? I hope it isn't serious!' she exclaimed.

'It's measles.' The young constable was repressing a schoolboy grin. 'He never had it when he was a kid seemingly. He'll be off for three weeks. Can I help you?'

Sister Joan bit her lip. With both Alan Mill and Petrie away the two who counted her as a helpful friend weren't available. Reporting her suspicions about the identity of the man found dead in the old chapel would inevitably lead to further questions. It would be impossible to keep Caroline Hayes's name out of it, and that might well alert her brother-in-law if he had anything to hide. The last image she had had of him, a very large suitcase in one bony hand, flashed into her head.

'I understand that a young woman called Caroline Hayes made some enquiries here a few days ago. I wondered if that could be confirmed.'

'I wasn't here then, Sister,' the constable said. 'I'll see if I can find anything in the book – oh, Constable Brown might know. Was there a Miss Hayes making enquiries here a couple of days back?'

Constable Brown, a part-time policeman fighting the notion of retirement and holding, according to Detective Sergeant Mill, ideas about women that would've been politically incorrect in the Ark, gave Sister Joan a brusque nod and said, 'She came in two – no, three days ago. I don't think anything was put in the book. Not really important enough.'

'Thank you, Constable Brown.' Sister Joan gave him her

sweetest smile, aware that it would be completely lost on him. 'Give my best wishes to Constable Petrie if you see him. Say I hope he'll soon be fit again. Good morning.'

Her information would have to wait until either Detective Sergeant Mill or Constable Petrie was around. She consoled herself with the thought that the death had been a natural one and that it was probably an advantage not to alert the authorities just yet.

Having made her purchases, not forgetting Sister Gabrielle's aspirins, she walked back in the direction of the station, in time to see the now familiar figure of Michael Peter approaching her.

'Good morning, Mr Peter.' She raised her voice slightly to attract his attention, since he was walking slowly and musingly, his eyes on the ground.

'Good morning – Sister!' His head jerked up. 'Haven't we met before?'

'I came into your shop.'

'Yes, of course. So you did! Sister – Joan.'

'I'm afraid I asked some rather impertinent questions.'

'Oh, I'm sure you didn't intend—' His bony fingers waved vaguely and were still. 'You expressed an interest in painting, I seem to be remembering.'

'And you told me about your costume exhibition.'

'Yes, so I did. The shop will be open this afternoon but I won't have time. After that it will be open again on Monday. If you care to come in then?'

'If I can. My movements aren't exactly under my control,' Sister Joan said.

'Religious discipline, yes. Well, any day you can obtain permission I shall be only too happy to show you round. The costumes are original, you know.'

'Yes, you told me. It sounds very interesting.'

'Oh, while I remember!' Walking on, he stopped and turned suddenly. 'Mrs Rufus, my housekeeper, asked to be remembered to you. It made quite a little change for her to have a visitor. We are rather isolated.'

He turned and walked on again, greying head bent again,

ungloved hands swinging free, unencumbered by luggage of any kind.

There was no sign of life as she passed the schoolhouse. She wondered if Caroline Hayes still sat, huddled on the chair, the half-finished mug of cold tea in her hands, her mind ordering her to take the positive action her lack of courage denied.

'May I make a telephone call, Mother Dorothy?' Having delivered the various small commissions with which she had been entrusted she caught up with the prioress on her way across the main hall.

'Another one!' Mother Dorothy gave her a disapproving look through her steel-framed spectacles. 'A matter of extreme urgency, I suppose?'

'Some research I'm doing,' Sister Joan said.

'Not for the police? You are obligated to tell me if you are needed to give any such help in your capacity as citizen.'

'No, Mother Dorothy,' Sister Joan said truthfully. 'Not for the police.'

'Would a letter serve as well?'

'I suppose so.'

'Then write a letter,' Mother Dorothy said briskly. 'You have time before lunch. Lilith would enjoy a gallop to the mailbox.'

'Yes, Mother Dorothy.' Sister Joan went swiftly into the chapel wing and up the stairs to the library where Sister David was working.

'Did you want a book, Sister?'

Peering over the pile of books and papers that always surrounded her Sister David looked like a fourth former caught after lights out. That she was in her thirties, held several impressive degrees in Ancient Languages and read St Thomas Aquinas for fun wasn't apparent from her timid, anxious-to-please manner.

'Do you have the address of St Catherine's House in London?' Sister Joan asked.

'Second shelf down of the reference section. On the right.'

Blessedly uncurious Sister David went back to her translation.

Sister Joan found the book, noted the address and the price

of birth certificates and wrote the necessary request enclosing a cheque which cleaned out her modest savings account except for three pounds.

The post went at two on Saturdays. She hurried downstairs, borrowed a stamp from Sister Mary Concepta and hastened to saddle up Lilith. Not until she was cantering over the moor towards the mailbox which stood at the top of the long slope leading down to the estate which spread in a rash of flats and houses round the perimeter of the higher ground did she realize she'd forgotten to put on her jeans. She posted her letter, turned to remount again, and remembered the letter that Caroline Hayes had given her to read. She led the pony a little way back, tethered her loosely to a tree stump and sat on a nearby slab of rock to read the letter.

The handwriting was round and childish with several of the letters left unjoined and the small case b frequently substituted for d. Crystal probably had some degree of dyslexia, she reflected, smoothing out the folded sheet.

The address of the Peter house was written at the top right-hand side with a date in late March immediately beneath it.

'*Dear Dad and Caroline,*' ran the salutation.

Thank you for your nice letter, Dad. I'm glad that you're feeling a bit more the thing. Please let me know when you're going into hospital for more tests and how it turns out for you. We have had very wet weather here, pouring with rain most days, and quite chilly in the mornings. Sometimes I wish I was anywhere but here. Michael likes the quiet but it gets on my nerves and Mrs Rufus isn't any company. She's a big pain in the arse to be frank. I've been dreaming a lot lately. I keep dreaming of Mum, and the flowers we put on her grave, but in the dream it's my grave with my name on it. Sometimes I walk over to a little chapel near the house and just sit there, hoping she might come, but she never does, of course. Sorry to sound a bit down, but I miss you both like crazy. I'm going to get Michael to shut up his stupid shop for a few days and bring me to see you.

Regards and Lots of Love from us both.

Crystal.

Sister Joan read the letter over again, frowning as the subtext became clearer. Crystal Peter hadn't been a happy or contented wife. She sounded lonely and apprehensive, and certainly not as well educated as might have been expected of the wife of a cultured man like the antique dealer. On the other hand middle-aged bachelors often adored young girls with sweet smiles and wheedling ways. It was usually a recipe for disaster.

She jotted down the address on the front of the envelope, remounted Lilith, and rode back towards the convent. Odd, but she'd never realized before that the convent itself stood roughly at the centre of a landscape cross with the estate over on the north, the town on the south, the Romany camp and the river away to the west and on the east, beyond the schoolhouse, the wilder slopes interspersed with small patches of arable land and the long, low house where Michael Peter and his young wife had lived. Now why had the past tense come into her head? She looked around, seeing the high folds and billows of grass and peat and tumbled rocks that hid each quarter of the landscape from its neighbours. Only in the convent was it possible to be centred.

She made luncheon by the skin of her teeth, sinking into her place on the long wooden bench two seconds ahead of the prioress. Lunch was a meal to be eaten silently after which the community returned to work until the lecture at four. Over in the postulancy Sister Hilaria, the novice mistress, was training the solitary postulant the convent boasted, though quality was better than quantity and Sister Bernadette seemed like a nice girl. How she managed to confine her conversation to dialogues with Mother Dorothy and Sister Hilaria, Sister Joan couldn't imagine. Then she grinned, recalling her own postulancy in the London house when she too had been forbidden to speak to or mix with the professed sisters. She'd got through it, though she'd had companions at the same stage of religious training as herself whilst poor Bernadette had nobody.

'Share the joke, Sister.' Sister Gabrielle looked at her invitingly as they went down the stairs again.

'I was wondering how I managed to get through my

postulancy without breaking the rules of silence,' Sister Joan said.

'It's a question I've often considered,' Sister Gabrielle said dryly. 'I came to the conclusion they probably got so used to your chatter they simply didn't hear it any longer. Mother Dorothy says that you've been running around making telephone calls and posting letters. Helping out the local constabulary again, are we?'

'Not this time.'

'Nevertheless I'd lay odds that you're up to something.' The old nun sent her a shrewd look from beneath heavy white eyebrows. 'Need any advice?'

'I don't think so, Sister, but may I come to you if I do?'

'Well, you've nice manners anyway!' Sister Gabrielle said with a bark of mirth. 'A word of advice from me would send you scurrying in the opposite direction and don't pretend otherwise! The young always know better than their elders and that's right and proper.'

'I was wondering why a young woman would marry a man twice her age.'

'Is the man rich?'

'Fairly comfortable, I'd say. That was a very cynical remark, Sister!'

'I'm eighty-seven years old,' Sister Gabrielle said placidly. 'I've the right to be cynical. Of course there's no accounting for love. It can strike anybody at any time, they say, though it never landed on me unfortunately. It would've been rather nice to congratulate myself on my good sense in giving up a lesser love for a greater one, but the truth is that I always wanted to be a nun.'

'That must've made things simple,' Sister Joan began.

'Not really,' Sister Gabrielle said. 'My father was a Methodist minister.'

'Oh Lord!'

'Oh Lord indeed! We didn't even know any Catholics so what gave me the idea of being a nun remains a mystery. God must've decided that I'd do less harm in the religious life than out in the world I suppose. Anyway it took a lot of persuasion before he would countenance my taking instruction in the Faith and I was twenty-four when he finally agreed that I had a vocation. No, nothing's simple, Sister.'

She patted Sister Joan on the arm and limped away.

'Did you post your letter, Sister?' Mother Dorothy bore down, an odd word to think of when the prioress was scarcely taller than herself, Sister Joan thought.

'Yes, Mother Dorothy.'

'Have you anything planned for this afternoon?'

'I'll go where I'm most needed,' Sister Joan said promptly.

'This is a difficult period for you,' Mother Dorothy said with unexpected sympathy. 'All the other sisters have their allotted tasks and you merely fill in where help is required. I did consider appointing you assistant novice mistress as you know, but with only one postulant at the moment you would have been somewhat superfluous.'

'Yes, Mother Dorothy.'

'And no doubt you feel somewhat superfluous as it is.' The eyes behind the steel-framed spectacles twinkled unexpectedly. 'Try to look at it in a more positive way, Sister. You can devote more time to the act of adoration which is central to our lives. The others are often pressed for time and cannot spend as long in private meditation as they wish, so you could supply the lack.'

'It isn't easy to spend hours in the chapel when other people need your help,' Sister Joan said.

'You can help them by being in the chapel surely?'

'I know, but sometimes practical help is required too.'

'Then give it.' Mother Dorothy gave her a long thoughtful look. 'I ask no questions, Sister, but if there's something on your mind, some task unfulfilled, see to it.'

'Thank you, Mother Prioress.'

But her priorities had been spelled out. She went off to pull on her wellingtons and join Sister Martha in the garden. Luther was there, scything the long grass that had sprung up during the heavy spring rains, his long face splitting into a delighted grin as he saw her.

'Good afternoon, Sister! I haven't got no rose for you,' he said apologetically.

'Sister Martha shared her rose with all of us. How are you, Luther?'

'I seen a lady,' he said confidingly. 'In Brother Cuthbert's house.'

'Brother Cuthbert went to stay in Scotland. The lady you saw is staying in the old schoolhouse for a week or so. You didn't bother her, did you?'

Luther who had once been committed to a mental hospital because of his habit of following women in a manner that was certainly annoying and which several of them had interpreted as threatening, shook his head.

'It's bad to follow ladies,' he said solemnly. 'It frightens them.'

'So you didn't bother her?'

'No, ma'am. No indeed!' He shook his head and looked grave. 'I like it here. I don't want ever to go back there again! No, Sister, I only saw her at the window and then she ducked down quick.'

'That sounds like a funny thing to do,' Sister Martha, on her knees as she grubbed up weeds, looked up puzzled.

'I believe she wants to be quite private,' Sister Joan said.

'Too much of the world pressing in on her.' Sister Martha nodded, and bent again to her work. 'Still she might like a bit of company. Is she catering for herself?'

'Sort of half and half,' Sister Joan said.

'I've some nice salad greens,' Sister Martha said. 'Perhaps you'd like to go over and give her some. Luther and I can manage fine here.'

'Thank you, Sister.'

Riding Lilith over the moor to the schoolhouse was much more enjoyable than grubbing up weeds, Sister Joan reflected, hurrying to pull on her jeans under the full, ankle-length skirts of her habit and find a large bag for the greens. It would also give her the chance to return the letter from Crystal. Until she heard from St Catherine's House there wasn't much more she could do.

The little schoolhouse looked as deserted as Luther had said. She slipped from Lilith's broad back and unhooked the large bag of onions and lettuce and cress that Sister Martha had provided and went briskly to the door, raising her voice as she knocked.

'It's only Sister Joan! Anyone in?'

For a moment there was no answer then footsteps sounded within and the key was turned.

'Are you by yourself?' Caroline asked, opening the door a bare two inches.

'Yes, of course. I've brought some salad to add to your supplies.'

The door opened wider and Caroline stood aside, pulling a cardigan round her shoulders, its colour the same drab brown as the rest of her outfit.

'Is anything the matter?' Sister Joan carried the bag into the living-room and looked with concern at the younger woman's white face and dark shadowed eyes.

'A man was prowling around,' Caroline said. 'A very peculiar looking man. He came right up to the window and tried to look in, but I ducked down and just prayed that he wouldn't see me. I was scared that Michael Peter had sent him.'

'That was Luther,' Sister Joan said. 'He's a mite simple but perfectly harmless. He's nothing to do with your brother-in-law. Anyway why should Michael Peter send someone over to check whether or not you're here? He doesn't even know you're in the district.'

'You haven't told anyone?'

'I told Mother Dorothy that a Miss Hayes had taken the place for a week because she wanted some peace and quiet,' Sister Joan said patiently.

'You didn't mention—?'

'No, I promised that I'd say nothing. Look, here's some salad for you. It needs washing but it's all home grown. You are eating, aren't you?' She looked sharply at the other, anxiety creeping over her as she noted the twitching fingers of the thin hands. The girl looked close to a breakdown of some sort.

'I'm being stupid,' Caroline said. 'I know I'm being stupid. Coming down here like this and not having the guts to face Michael Peter and demand to see my sister! I know I'm being stupid.'

'Not so stupid,' Sister Joan said quickly. 'You haven't heard from Crystal for over two months and then you get the initial telling you she needs help, and the letter you gave me to read – she sounds very nervous. If she was my sister I'd be alarmed too.'

'Do you have a sister? I mean a real sister?' Caroline asked.

'Only two brothers.'

'Then you can't really understand,' Caroline said, picking up the bag of salad and clutching it to her like a barrier. 'Crystal and I are devoted. We always lived our own lives, of course, because we're very different but there's nobody else in the world who understands me so well, not even Dad. We absolutely adore each other, Sister Joan, and if anything's happened to her I simply won't be able to bear it!'

SIX

The rest of Saturday had passed quietly enough, with minds concentrated on the general confession which followed the benediction. Sister Joan had returned the letter to Caroline Hayes and urged her to get some rest.

'That's all I am doing, Sister!' Caroline's eyes were wide and strained. 'I sit here and go over and over things in my mind. I ought to be doing something but I don't know what to do. I have this awful feeling that if I do move then something dreadful will happen.'

'Look, tomorrow's Sunday,' Sister Joan said. 'We have the afternoon largely to ourselves to read, write letters, take a walk. I'll ride over to the house and have a word with Mrs Rufus. Then I'll come over and let you know if I've found anything out.'

'You won't let her know that I'm in the area?'

'No, of course not, but Mrs Rufus isn't likely to do you any harm!'

'She works for Michael Peter, doesn't she?' Caroline said tensely. 'In one of her letters Crystal said that she told him absolutely everything that went on. If he knew that I was here he might come looking for me.'

'To do what?' Sister Joan demanded. 'Look, he seems to be spreading it about that your sister has gone off on a touring holiday with you and the parents. We know that isn't true because you're here and your mother died some time ago anyway. This time you could go to the police and get a hearing.'

'And Michael Peter would explain it all away,' Caroline said. 'He'd deny having said anything to you, or he'd twist it about somehow so that you ended up looking a fool, and then he'd be on his guard and we wouldn't be able to find out anything else at all. Please wait a couple more days!'

She had agreed unwillingly and ridden back to the convent with a weight on her mind that would, she knew, become intolerable if it wasn't soon resolved. Not until the recreation which was shorter on Saturday nights did the chance come to unburden herself. Sister Gabrielle, who usually struggled up to meals and recreation even when her joints were inflamed, excused herself.

'I'm perfectly well,' she said quickly in response to Sister Perpetua's anxious enquiry. 'I merely feel like a bit of a change, that's all. Sister Mary Concepta will keep you in good order until chapel. Sister Joan, at this moment what I crave most in the world is a nice mug of cocoa, made with milk and plenty of sugar.'

'I'll ask Mother Dorothy if you can have it,' Sister Joan said.

'But ask Sister Teresa to make it,' Sister Gabrielle said. 'You're bound to leave lumps in it. I've not recovered from the last jug of custard you produced when you were doing the cooking!'

'She's not ill, is she?' Mother Dorothy asked when the request was put.

'I don't think so, Mother Prioress, though her rheumatism pains her more than she'll admit,' Sister Joan said.

'By all means let her have her cocoa then and she's excused from this evening's period of recreation. If she seems to want company then stay with her.'

'Yes, Mother Dorothy.'

Having duly received the cocoa from Sister Teresa, Sister Joan went into the infirmary which was the only room in the building where a fire was permitted. Sister Gabrielle was seated by it, her old eagle face turned to the door as Sister Joan came in.

'Ah! Cocoa!' Her tone was triumphant. 'Did Sister Teresa make it?'

'Yes, Mother told me to tell her to get it ready.'

'It looks rather hot,' Sister Gabrielle said, peering over the rim of the mug. 'Would you be kind enough to drink some of it yourself before giving it to me? Sister Teresa has filled it rather too full.'

The drink was hot, sweet and comforting. Sipping it, Sister Joan caught Sister Gabrielle's eye on her and found herself laughing.

'What's going on, Sister?' she asked. 'This cocoa was made for you, not me.'

'Drink some more and I'll finish it up,' Sister Gabrielle ordered. 'Now, sit down and tell me why your mind is jumping about like a cat on a hot tin roof.'

'Sister!'

'I've read my modern literature,' Sister Gabrielle said, accepting the half emptied mug. 'You're thirty-nine years old and at that age many in the religious life wake up to the fact that life means life, that they won't be finding a husband or raising a family in this world. And you're in the unfortunate position of not having a definite job assigned to you. So if you feel like talking about it—?'

'My mind is troubled,' Sister Joan said, 'but it's got nothing to do with sexual frustration, honestly. I have a problem, and I know what I ought to do as a good citizen, what Mother Dorothy would tell me to do, but I'm not sure.'

'About what?'

'You heard about the man I found in that old chapel over on the east side of the moor?'

'Yes, of course. Mother Dorothy said he'd died of a heart attack. Do you know who he was?'

'I believe so.'

Swiftly Sister Joan outlined the events since.

'I ought to tell the police but if I do that then Caroline Hayes's presence in the district will come out and since Michael Peter was the son-in-law he'll obviously be informed too. Then he's bound to realize that he's under suspicion and take steps to cover his tracks. I simply don't know what's best to do and with Detective Sergeant Mill on holiday and

Constable Petrie down with the measles—'

'You haven't got the local police force in your pocket any longer,' Sister Gabrielle finished. 'This man who died. Why wasn't his identity discovered at once?'

'Because there was nothing on him to identify him.'

'Can't they check dental records, hospital records?'

'Since it was a death due to natural causes I don't think very extensive investigations have been carried out.'

'And of course Detective Sergeant Mill wasn't there to do anything. Well, my dear, if the poor man had nothing on him in the way of identification then I'd say he was anxious to keep his identity a secret, wouldn't you?' Sister Gabrielle said. 'If the sister is worried about Crystal Peter's whereabouts then surely the father is too. So he encourages his other daughter to go off for a break with her friends and comes down to Cornwall instead of going into hospital for treatment as he's supposed to do. He removes anything on his person that might reveal who he is and sets off for Michael Peter's house, perhaps intending to represent himself as a fellow down on his luck and looking for work. He starts to feel ill, and goes into the old chapel to sit down, and dies there, his mission unfulfilled.'

'You think I ought to say nothing for the present? But Caroline still thinks that he's alive.'

'Bad news will always keep for a little,' Sister Gabrielle said. 'Right now she's desperately concerned for her sister and afraid that Michael Peter might discover she's in the district. "Sufficient unto the day is the evil thereof". And what are you going to do about it?'

'I don't know,' Sister Joan said. 'This isn't an official case. It isn't a case at all really. Nobody's been reported missing, nobody's been murdered.'

'But this young woman came to you because she'd seen your name in a newspaper article. She asked you to help her. I think you should do. Go over and see this Mrs Rufus. She probably knows a great deal about her employer. Have you checked on any part of Caroline Hayes's story?'

'I've sent off to St Catherine's House for details of both sisters. I asked them to reply urgently so hopefully I'll get a letter during the week.'

'Then go and see Mrs Rufus,' Sister Gabrielle said.

'Oh Lord!' In the act of rising Sister Joan clapped her hand to her mouth. 'My wits really are woolgathering! Mrs Rufus doesn't work at the house on Sundays!'

'Do you know where she does live?'

'She said something about having a house over on the estate. Anyway she'd think it a bit peculiar if I went looking for her on her day off. I shall have to leave it until Monday.'

'Go back to the old chapel and poke about there for a bit. You might,' said Sister Gabrielle with relish, 'find some clues.'

'And turn myself into Sister Sherlock!' Sister Joan said. 'You've been a great help, Sister.'

'The cocoa helped,' Sister Gabrielle said with a twinkle in her eye. 'You ought to learn not to get so personally involved with other people's problems, child.'

'I know.'

'On the other hand,' Sister Gabrielle said thoughtfully, 'the fellow who was mugged in the Gospels wouldn't have fared very well if the good Samaritan had simply rushed past on his way to the temple to worship his Creator! Shall we go into chapel now?'

Yes, it had been a peaceful day and she had woken on Sunday morning with a lively feeling of anticipation.

'Is it all right if I leave the grounds this afternoon Mother Dorothy?' Asking for the customary permission she received a brisk nod.

'You'll be looking in on our temporary tenant, Sister?' Mother Dorothy said.

'Later on, yes, Mother.'

'I hope she's not finding it too peaceful,' Mother Dorothy said, as she turned back into her parlour.

On her way out she came across Sister Hilaria, with the pink-smocked, white-bonneted postulant, Bernadette, tagging along meekly.

'We are picking wild flowers, Sister Joan,' Sister Hilaria said. 'We shall decorate the postulancy with them and meditate on the meaning of beauty.'

Her rather prominent eyes were more accustomed to survey-
ing the clouds than the earth, Sister Joan thought, with a tremor
of affectionate amusement. As a novice mistress she gave her
charges an example that was hard to follow but which Mother
Dorothy insisted would act as an inspiration.

At her heels the solitary postulant the convent at present
boasted cast down her eyes in the approved manner but not
before she had favoured Sister Joan with the hint of a wink. Life
would liven up when Bernadette joined the novitiate, Sister Joan
thought, leaving them to their wild-flower gathering along the
borders of the shrubbery and giving Lilith her head as she
cantered out on to the moor.

There was no sign of life from the schoolhouse. Was Caroline
sleeping or simply sitting, eyes wide and frightened, ears
pricked for the threat of an unfamiliar footfall? There was no
point in disturbing her, anyway, until there was some definite
news to impart. She rode past the building and headed the pony
in the direction of the swells and hollows that concealed the old
chapel.

This afternoon it was as deserted as usual, its roof partly fallen
in, the long grass that grew up around the stone walls waving in
the breeze, though whether in welcome or warning it was
difficult to tell. She dismounted and went inside, treading with
care over the heaps of mossy rock and fallen stone.

Sister Gabrielle had suggested looking for clues. Sister Joan
doubted if any clues remained to be found. All she had was the
torn strip of paper with the name and number of Michael Peter
on it. Presumably Mr Hayes, if he was the man who had died
here, had found it in a pocket he believed he had emptied and
hastily scuffed it down into the dirt with the heel of his shoe.
Clearly he'd been on his way to the Peter house and that
suggested that his appearance was unknown to his son-in-law.
Caroline had mentioned a photograph of herself and Crystal
together which made it impossible to hide her identity should
she run into Michael Peter. Apparently there was no photograph of Mr Hayes. Which might mean anything or nothing,
Sister Joan mused, and stiffened as a little fall of pebbles outside
the entrance heralded a newcomer.

Turning slowly, she saw the tall figure of the man she had been thinking about stoop beneath the lintel and straighten up, staring at her.

'Is it—? The light is not so good in here,' he said.

'It's Sister Joan, Mr Peter.' She went forward, raising her voice slightly.

'Sister Joan? Ah, yes. We seem to keep running into each other, Sister.'

'I brought our pony, Lilith, out for her exercise,' Sister Joan said. 'This is a curious old building, isn't it?'

'Eighteenth century. It was a Methodist meeting house until the middle of last century, and then a bigger chapel was built on the outskirts of town and this fell gradually into decay. Such a pity when that's allowed to happen, don't you think?'

'Yes, indeed.' Sister Joan stepped past him into the open air. 'Our own convent was once a handsome estate, the property of the Tarquin family. We try to look after it but money's always pretty tight.'

'But the place is lived in,' Michael Peter said. 'Houses require company, Sister. I have always believed that.'

'Yes.' She moved to Lilith's head, reaching for the reins, wishing that he didn't loom so as if he were gathering himself together to spring.

'I don't suppose you would accept a cup of coffee?' he said, not springing anywhere but looking anxious. 'Mrs Rufus doesn't come in on Sundays but I can make a very decent cup of coffee and she made some buns yesterday.'

'A cup of coffee would be very nice,' Sister Joan said.

She'd prayed hard for guidance that morning, for a way forward to be shown to her, and it looked as if God had been paying attention.

'Come along then. It isn't a very long walk – but you've already taken it! I forgot. You found that unfortunate tramp in the chapel here. Did I interrupt you? Were you praying for his soul?'

'Not exactly,' Sister Joan said, resolving to do so at the first available opportunity. 'Mrs Rufus told you about that?'

'Mrs Rufus tells me a very great deal.' He gave a slightly

twisted grin. 'Of course, she's alone all day so when I run her home she fills in the drive with words. Long streams of words about the most unimportant details of her day. It's very wearing.'

'Surely she has your wife to talk to?' Sister Joan ventured.

'My – oh, yes, Crystal.' He shot her a startled look. 'But my wife's away at present, touring France with her family. I believe I already mentioned that.'

'Yes you did. You haven't heard anything?'

'No. I don't expect to yet. These two fields also belong to me. I grow corn in them or rather a local farmer rents them to grow corn in. The soil isn't very fertile but the grain seems to do fairly well. Are you interested in conservation, Sister?'

She longed to reply she was more interested in finding his wife at that moment but murmured politely in response and was treated to a long discourse of infinite tedium on the benefits of organic farming as they traversed the two fields and approached the long, low, stone house with its neatly planted rockery.

'Is your house old?' she found the chance to say as they entered the front door, leaving Lilith tethered to the gate.

'Almost a hundred years old,' he said. 'It was a farmhouse but the people moved to the city and I bought it and extended it. Personally I hoped to maintain its character both inside and out but housekeepers demand electrical gadgets and plastic stuff.'

'It's still a lovely house.'

'Thank you.' He looked pleased. 'I spent a long time over the renovations and redecoration. My mother was still alive when we moved here, and she always took a keen interest in the place. Now, make yourself comfortable and I'll get the coffee.'

He loped out into the hall and Sister Joan perched herself at the table and folded her hands sedately in her lap. Every nerve in her body longed to rush through the house looking for what Sister Gabrielle had optimistically termed clues, but she forced herself to stillness and outward tranquillity. There was simply no point in alerting Michael Peter to the possibility that she was on an investigation.

'Here we come!' He came in with a tray on which a silver coffee jug with cups, sugar bowl and cream jug were set. 'Will you do the honours, Sister, while I get the buns?' He strode kitchenwards again, while she poured the coffee, savouring the fragrant aroma, admiring the fluted china with its border of gold rosebuds.

'Sugar but no cream for me. Thank you, Sister. They're raspberry buns. Mrs Rufus makes them from a recipe my mother gave her.'

He sat down opposite her.

'Mrs Rufus was here then? When your mother was alive, I mean?'

'She came part-time,' he said, sipping his drink. 'Of course her husband was still alive then and so she didn't work full-time. Mother was very feeble towards the end and really ought to have had a trained nurse but Mr Rufus died quite suddenly and Mrs Rufus agreed to come full-time, except on Sundays when I was free to take care of Mother myself. The two of them got on splendidly together, but then everybody adored Mother. She knew more about the antique business than anyone I ever met and she wore her great knowledge so lightly. You'd have loved her, Sister Joan. Right up to the end she was quite sound of mind, you know. Sharp as a needle when it came to a bargain. Do have a bun – or isn't it allowed?'

'I don't think it'll be a hanging matter when I tell Mother Dorothy,' Sister Joan said, biting into the feathery sponge and feeling the sensual trickle of raspberry preserve on her tongue.

'I do like to see a lady eat.' Michael Peter gave her the wide smile that looked more like a grin of pain. 'My wife – Crystal enjoys her food. She has a very sweet tooth, and she's one of those fortunate ladies who can eat anything and not gain an ounce.'

'She'll be enjoying the food in France then.'

'In France? Oh, yes indeed. That should be quite a gourmet treat. More coffee, Sister?'

She was sure she'd exceeded her permitted quota for the day but so far she'd found out nothing.

'Thank you, Mr Peter. I was just admiring the cups.'

'Not antiques,' he said, watching her refill her cup. 'Mother had them made for her specially by a friend. It was her seventieth birthday and her name, of course, was Rose. Such a lovely gentle name.'

'Like Crystal,' Sister Joan said.

'Crystal.' He echoed the name after her, his hand suspended in the act of raising his cup to his lips. 'Bright and sparkling, many faceted, and delicate. Wouldn't you say?'

'Did your mother—?' Sister Joan hesitated.

'Oh, I didn't meet Crystal until five years after Mother passed away,' he said. 'No, another woman here all the time wouldn't have suited Mother at all. Not living here as part of our little family so to speak. No, we were very happy here but then Mother passed on and even with Mrs Rufus looking after everything so splendidly it wasn't the same. Nobody to chat with in the evenings.'

'Where did you meet?'

'At a trade fair. She was one of the hostesses, giving out the sales lists, directing people to the various stands. We talked a great deal. She listened more than talked if I'm to be honest. I was very – taken. Yes, very taken. Most thankfully she seemed equally taken with me. I suppose I represented a father figure to her, poor girl. Her own relations with her parents were not ideal. They favoured the sister, you see.'

'You haven't met them?'

He shook his head.

'They were abroad when we married – in Canada, I believe. It was a very quiet wedding. Registry office. You don't approve of that.'

'Not for Catholics,' Sister Joan admitted. 'But you make the vows to each other so it probably doesn't really matter where they're made.'

'As you say, Sister.' He took a bun and bit into it.

'And she still went off on holiday with them?' Sister Joan said.

'I beg your pardon?'

'She didn't have a good relationship with her parents but she went on holiday with them?'

'To France, yes.' He stared at her for a moment. 'Ah, yes, I see what you mean. To tell you the truth, Sister, I was a little surprised about that myself, but Crystal said it was an opportunity for them to get together and talk, really talk. And of course she was always on good terms with her sister. Wait! I've a photograph of them.'

He leapt up rather like a jack-in-the-box and went out of the room. Sister Joan drank the last of her coffee and waited, hearing his feet padding down the stairs and across the shining hall.

'Here we are!' he said. 'It was taken a couple of years back. Rather a nice one, I think, don't you?'

'Very nice,' Sister Joan agreed, the two young women, had arms linked affectionately, as they faced the camera. Crystal was fair-haired with a short, curly style and a sweet, guileless face – not a face with much strength of character, she guessed, but one that would certainly captivate a lonely, middle-aged bachelor. Not one of whom his dear sweet mother Rose would have approved. Next to her sister Caroline looked serious and a little disapproving.

'She's very lovely, isn't she?' He took back the photograph and looked at it. 'I wish we had had more photographs taken – of ourselves together, for example. However—'

'You don't have any snaps of her mum and dad? I love looking at family snapshots,' Sister Joan said brightly.

'I'm afraid not. Just this one. Crystal wanted us to begin a whole new life together, unencumbered by the past. Well, Sister, I mustn't keep you from your religious duties.'

'I've outstayed my welcome,' she apologized, rising hastily, 'but I found it a very pleasant change to sit and chat. In fact I had been thinking of riding over here today anyway to call on Mrs Rufus – she was very kind in letting me use the phone the other day—'

'For which you insisted on paying. Quite unnecessarily so, Sister.'

'And then I remembered she'd mentioned she didn't work here on Sundays and as I don't have her address—'

'Number fifty, Walnut Avenue. It's just behind the sports centre on the new estate.'

'Well, perhaps another time then.'

'Or call here,' he invited. 'As I told you Mrs Rufus does find the day rather long without any company. You haven't forgotten about my little exhibition?'

'The costumes, no. I shall look forward to it.'

'I shall enjoy showing you round. Perhaps on Tuesday?'

'I'll ask Mother Prioress for leave.'

'And if I have to go away on business,' he said, 'then I shall leave the key to the extension to the shop at the hairdresser's next door. You must feel free to look round by yourself. Indeed I suspect you might even appreciate it all more if you went round by yourself and soaked up the atmosphere.'

'May I use your toilet before I start back?' Sister Joan broke in to ask.

'The toilet? Oh, of course! Forgive me, Sister, but one doesn't usually think of nuns having to – it's the door on the half landing upstairs.'

'Thank you.'

The stairs curved round on to the half landing and then curved round again to a long passage with doors opening off it along one side. Sister Joan wished she could explore further. Were Crystal's clothes still in the wardrobe? Had she and her elderly husband even shared the same room or had the marriage been one of companionship only? In her mind she was trying to build up a picture of the pretty young woman who would marry a man like Michael Peter, but the pictures wavered and shrank.

She went into the toilet and closed the door. It comprised a shower cubicle as well as a basin and a lavatory, the floor tiled, warm pink shading to cream on the shower curtain and a window blind. It had a luxurious air very much in contrast to the strictly utilitarian bathrooms at the convent. A shelf held aromatherapy oils, talcum powder and bath crystals. She imagined sponging herself down with the huge sponge that hung from a hook on the wall, spraying herself with the cologne – no, it wasn't sex that she missed, she thought with amusement. It was creamy white soap and bath oil and all the luxuries of Delilah.

Flushing the lavatory she jumped slightly as the noise momentarily deafened her. The old outgrown childish superstition that if you flushed the loo with the door closed the ceiling would fall down jumped into her mind, and she took a hasty step towards the door, her foot catching on a wastepaper basket in the corner. Fortunately it was made of wicker, causing no noise as it tilted and spilled its contents on the floor.

'No harm done.' She knelt to pick up the odd rolls of tissue paper, realizing that it wasn't for waste but for extra supplies.

They were pushed down inside one of the plump rolls of pink tissue. Sister Joan tugged them out with difficulty and stared at them as they lay on her palm: a credit card with the name John Hayes written neatly on the appropriate place, a man's watch with a broad leather strap and a fountain pen with the initials J.H. stencilled along the barrel. The inside of the toilet roll had been carefully scooped out to contain them. It really began to look as if that death in the abandoned chapel hadn't been natural after all.

SEVEN

Her dilemma was two-fold. If she went to the police then the whole story of Caroline's quest for her sister would have to be told and the dead man identified. Michael Peter, if he was the guilty party, would immediately cover his tracks. On the other hand what proof was there of any crime? The autopsy on the dead man had revealed an enlarged heart. Even if he were proved to be John Hayes there might have been a quite innocent reason for his credit card, watch and fountain pen to be hidden in the scooped-out middle of a toilet roll. He might've called at the house, left the things there himself, and been on his way back when he'd suffered his heart attack. But why leave the things hidden there anyway? As a silent threat to Michael Peter? Had he suspected his son-in-law of doing away with Crystal and, lacking positive proof, hoped to draw out the other into betraying himself? And ought she to tell Caroline Hayes or not?

It was illegal to withhold evidence from the police, but the various items didn't constitute evidence of anything in particular since officially no crime had been committed.

There was also the problem of whether or not to tell Caroline. That young woman presented a puzzle of her own. She had come down to Cornwall to enquire after her sister, had been worried enough to go to the police, had turned to herself for help on the strength of a newspaper article she had read, and now hid herself from view in the old schoolhouse and seemed terrified of her own shadow. No, it was better not to volunteer any information until after the reply to her enquiry at St

Catherine's House had arrived.

Having decided to remain undecided Sister Joan thrust what she had found into her capacious pocket and went, outwardly serene, down the stairs to where her host loomed by the open front door.

'Thank you again, Mr Peter,' she said. 'I look forward to seeing your costume display.'

'My pleasure, Sister.'

His handclasp was dry, rasping slightly like horsehair. She untied Lilith, mounted and set off, swerving westward and riding in a wide arc so that she had no need to pass too close to the schoolhouse.

'Did you visit Miss Hayes?' Mother Dorothy enquired as they trooped in for the cup of tea and buttered scone that was Sunday's treat.

'No, Mother Dorothy. I rode over to the Peter house. Mrs Rufus wasn't working there today but Mr Peter was kind enough to invite me in so I've had my tea and bun,' Sister Joan said.

'Very well, Sister.'

Sister Joan bit her lip as her superior moved way. So many compromises had to be made between absolute truth and expediency, she thought. Yet how could she confide fully in Mother Dorothy who would take the sensible, objective view and insist that all suspicions should be relayed in the proper quarter? Why on earth had Detective Sergeant Alan Mill chosen now to take his wife and two sons on holiday? He and his wife didn't even get on very well together, Sister Joan thought crossly. He had told her once briefly that his wife resented his job and didn't share his interests. There had already been a trial separation. She'd cut him short, wanting their own relationship to remain on the casual, semi-professional level, and he'd volunteered nothing about his private life since, but she missed his advice now, his keen intelligence, and the trust he placed in her opinions. As for Constable Petrie! Measles at his age!

'You look uncommonly irritable, child,' Sister Gabrielle remarked, her stick tapping the younger nun rather painfully on the shoulder.

'I'm supposed to be centring my life round the adoration of God,' Sister Joan said, 'and all I do is get involved in stupid situations that have nothing to do with me, and take up all my thinking. There are moments, Sister, when I feel completely useless.'

'Welcome to the human race,' Sister Gabrielle said and tapped her way onward up the stairs.

Sister Joan went along to the kitchen where she relieved her feelings by chopping the carrots and turnips ready for supper, uneasily aware that both Sister Teresa and Sister Marie would thank her gratefully and ignore her explanation that she was only letting off steam.

Monday morning brought renewed optimism as it usually did. Dressing in the early morning greyness of her cell, Sister Joan reminded herself that this morning her letter of enquiry to St Catherine's House where every birth, marriage and death since 1827 was logged would reach them, and hopefully fall into the hands of someone who recognized that 'urgent' meant 'speedy'.

Each day was a new day, she thought, opening her door and walking down the passage with a spring in her step and a cheerful expression on her face which earned a puzzled frown from little Sister David who considered that mornings should be taken more soberly.

Today it was Father Stephens who offered the mass, the first rays of sun haloing his head. Father Stephens offered the mass as if he had just been inspired to create the ritual, his rich voice rolling out the phrases like waterfalls of velvet and silk. His genuflections breathed adoration. If he held his pose long enough he might turn into a stained-glass figure, Sister Joan thought, and hastily got custody of her eyes and of an emerging giggle.

Father Stephens hardly ever stayed for a cup of coffee or a chat. This morning was no exception but as she came down from the scanty meal Mother Dorothy beckoned her into the parlour.

'I have an errand for you, Sister. Father Stephens has been saving part of his salary in order to buy a new communion cup as a surprise for Father Malone. The old one is only silver washed and Father Malone has often said how nice it would be to have real silver.'

'Father Malone said that?' Sister Joan arched an eyebrow.

'Or would have done had he thought of it,' Mother Dorothy said with a slight smile.

'I didn't think it mattered what the cup was made of. The outward aspect doesn't always have to reflect the inward intention.'

'Thank you, Sister. I asked you to undertake an errand and you kindly give me a lesson in theology,' Mother Dorothy said without emphasis.

'I beg your pardon, Reverend Mother.'

Prostrating herself to kiss the floor, Sister Joan wished she could learn to curb her too impulsive tongue.

'What you are thinking,' Mother Dorothy said, 'is that Father Stephens fancies having a real silver cup. Am I correct?'

'Forgive me, Mother, but I can't help feeling that Father Stephens is more interested sometimes in looking good on the altar than in adoring God,' Sister Joan said.

'I thought you more perceptive, Sister.' Mother Dorothy looked amused. 'Father Stephens is still very young in many ways. Of course he adores himself. If we don't then how can we adore God? We begin with the image and rise to the reality. Now are we going to have another choice bit of pseudotheological cant or are you ready to go on the errand?'

'Yes, Mother.'

'He intended to buy the cup himself but then it occurred to him that he might be noticed entering an expensive shop and the surprise would be spoiled. He wishes to have the children from the Children's Home present the cup when Father Malone next visits them, and to have his own part in it kept secret. He recently inherited a decent sized legacy from a great uncle and is spending part of it together with what he had already saved on the silver. Real silver, Sister. I have the money here. Seven hundred and fifty pounds. It won't buy a new cup of solid silver but it might purchase one that is secondhand but can be duly cleaned and consecrated. You have met Mr Peter who has rather a high-class establishment in town so I'm told. With your powers of persuasion you might be able to strike an equitable bargain with him. You have the whole morning ahead of you, Sister.'

Having had a heap of coals landed on her head Sister Joan, still somewhat crimson-faced, went out to the van, checked that it didn't require any petrol, firmly discouraged Alice from joining her, and drove away with mingled emotions of chagrin and pleasure. Father Stephens had a side to him that Mother Dorothy had divined and she herself had failed to credit. On the other hand she'd been entrusted with the task of buying the gift and expected to get a bargain. And she had the whole morning to herself.

There was no sign of any life as she drove past the schoolhouse. A small, treacherous hope that, after all, Caroline Hayes had decided to give up the search for her sister and gone quietly away woke in her. She drove on down into the town and parked in the station yard, climbing down in time to see Constable Brown walking towards her.

'Good morning, Constable.'

Her smile wavered slightly as he nodded his head stiffly, with a curt, 'Good morning, Sister. In town again?'

'Oh, we do get let out now and then,' she said.

'Yes,' said Constable Brown, looking as if in his view nuns ought to remain within their convent perpetually.

'How is Constable Petrie?' she enquired.

'Rather spotty as a matter of fact, Sister.' The policeman's manner became a trifle more yielding. 'Very kind of you to enquire. He'll be back on duty fairly soon, and fortunately we're in a quiet period just now.'

'No sudden crime wave?'

'Nothing for the public to bother their heads about,' he said snubbingly. 'Someone vandalized the chip shop last night but that happens every month, and some busybody came into the station with a suitcase of old clothes they swore they'd found on the embankment. Why they couldn't take it to the Lost and Found office at the station I'll never know. It means a lot of paperwork for us. I'll not keep you, Sister.'

It wasn't much use trying to charm Constable Brown, she decided, watching him walk away. Constable Brown divided women into wives who stayed home and cooked, bad women who went out and earned money for turning tricks, old ladies to be helped across roads, and religious women who ought to stay put and pray.

She walked back to the main street and turned into the side road where the antique shop was situated, next to the hairdresser's which advertised hair extensions. Sister Joan, whose own black hair, curling crisply over her head beneath the veil, had never grown past chin level shook her head mentally at the vagaries of fashion and went on into the shop.

'Good morning, Sister.' Michael Peter loomed from the back of the shop. 'You're my first customer this morning. I've not opened up the back premises yet.'

'Hopefully I'll look round your exhibition later,' Sister Joan said. 'Actually I'm here to buy something.'

'For the convent?'

His voice was politely interested but she sensed astonishment behind his eyes.

'Oh, normally we just couldn't afford your prices,' she said. 'No, a new communion cup is required for the church altar. It's a surprise for Father Malone, so please don't say anything. Mother Dorothy thought you might have a silver cup that could be used.'

'How much were you prepared to spend?' he asked.

Nothing vague about him now, Sister Joan thought with a mentally lifted eyebrow. His eyes and voice had sharpened, become worldly wise and shrewd.

'Seven hundred and fifty pounds,' she said.

'You'll scarcely get a real silver cup for that,' he said. 'I assume you want one that's chalice sized?'

'Yes please. Seven fifty is our top offer and we can't increase it. In fact Mother Dorothy is expecting something less expensive.'

'In silver.'

'In silver.' She fixed him with her dark-blue eyes.

'This isn't a charity shop you know,' he said coldly. 'It isn't a thrift shop either. And I'm not a Catholic, so you can hardly expect me to sell church ornaments.'

'You're not French either,' Sister Joan said, 'but you've a Napoleon writing desk over in the corner there.'

'As you say.'

He had stepped back and was staring at her. She had the idea that something had just changed. His bony hands had clenched at his sides and he thrust his greying head forward reminding her irresistibly of a snapping turtle. Then, without warning, he gave a rasping chuckle, the wide grin splitting his mouth.

'Upon my soul, Sister Joan, but you drive a hard bargain! I believe we do have a rather nice chalice – silver, of course. It was in a sale of church property a few years back. I don't usually purchase such things but this has some very nice chasing around the base – tiny oak leaves and apples. Unusual. You might care to take a look?'

'Not if I can't afford it,' she said cautiously.

'Nobody has enquired for anything similar since it came in,' Michael Peter said. 'I'd be willing to let it go for seven hundred and fifty pounds.'

'Perhaps I'd better have a look at it first,' Sister Joan said prudently.

'I'll get it for you.' He moved to a large cupboard and unlocked it. 'I'm a trifle delayed this morning, I'm afraid. Mrs Rufus didn't turn up. Most unlike her! I rang her number but there was no reply. She did mention some time ago that she might award herself a day out at Torquay with her friend, but I was probably thinking of something else. This is the cup. I'm not a churchgoer myself and certainly not high church, so you will be best fitted to pronounce on its suitability.'

He lifted down the gleaming chalice and set it on the table.

'It's beautiful.'

Sister Joan picked it up and looked at the delicate chasing around the base. It was also, even to her inexperienced eye, worth a lot more than £750.

'You have its provenance?' she asked.

'All duly receipted. I don't deal in stolen property, Sister.' His voice was gently chiding.

'No, of course not,' Sister Joan said, flushing. 'This is very generous of you, Mr Peter.'

'I'll find a container for it and let you have your sales receipt – also the other bits and pieces proving its provenance. It's to be a surprise, you say?'

'For Father Malone. You must know Father Malone. Everybody does.'

'I know very few people in the town,' he said. 'Mother was rather a shy, retiring lady who preferred to keep herself to herself. We never mingled much.'

'It must've been rather lonely for her.'

'No, not at all. Mrs Rufus came up nearly every day to do the heavy work and then in the evenings she had my company.'

'I meant for you,' Sister Joan said.

'Oh, I can do very nicely without the hum of conversation in my ears,' he said. 'Now, if you'll excuse me I must open up the extension. Have you time to look round before you go?'

'I've the whole morning.'

'Come along then!'

He replaced the chalice, now shrouded in a cardboard box in the cupboard, locked it, put a Closed sign on the front door and led the way up a narrow flight of stairs to the upper floor. Here, prints and paintings ranged around the walls, and larger pieces of furniture were set in groups as if to give the illusion that people actually sat on the chairs and hung up their garments in the massive wardrobes.

'Victorian,' Michael Peter said, nodding towards them. 'Not terribly popular in these days of small rooms but the craftsmanship is generally superb. This way.' He had drawn a curtain, deactivated an alarm and unlocked a wide door.

'Of course nothing here is for sale,' he said. 'It's more of a hobby for me than anything else. The idea of arranging my collection and of showing small selected parties over it is a comparatively new notion of mine. Children might be interested in it, don't you think?'

'I can't speak for them,' Sister Joan said, 'but I'm certainly fascinated!'

The extension was modern, joined on to the original building and tucked out of sight at the back. Within what was virtually a bare shell the Victorian age had been recreated, the space divided into long passages with small rooms, half walls enabling the visitor to look in at various scenes. Each setting provided a backdrop for a tableau of waxy figures, each one wigged and gowned, each one engaged in some activity into which their limbs were perpetually fixed. In one corner a small maidservant with streamers on her white cap was kneeling before an unlit fire, while her mistress stood behind her, apparently giving instructions. In another, a plump baby sat in a high carriage pram with a more smartly dressed nursemaid pushing the handles while a tall guardsman tried to catch her eye and an older child, wearing a tam o'shanter, was in the act of bowling a hoop as he ran past. Except that he would never move his waxen legs, never had moved them.

Sister Joan suppressed a sudden shiver. These figures were at the same time both too lifelike and not lifelike enough. Behind their bright eyes nothing human lived.

'Excuse me, please. I believe I hear someone at the door.' Michael Peter bobbed his head at her and retreated the way they had come.

Sister Joan walked on, pausing to look at a pretty bridal scene with the girl in a white crinoline festooned with roses and a poke bonnet shielding her face with its downcast eyes. At her side the groom stood stiffly, and two or three wedding guests raised champagne glasses in a little huddle at the side.

She walked on again, her footsteps silent on the thick underlay that covered the floor. She was in a larger room, with no wall separating her from the scene. Figures in black, two women wearing long black veils and holding lacy black handkerchiefs, were close enough for her to touch. On a long oak table, supine in an open coffin lined with white silk, a girl with long fair ringlets lay, arms crossed and a silken rose between her colourless fingers.

Reluctantly, drawn against her will, Sister Joan walked over and looked down at the recumbent figure. It was a beautifully staged tableau, meant to be touching, but it wasn't touching. It was macabre and the more so because the girl in the coffin had never lived at all, and the silent mourners had no hearts to feel.

'From birth to death,' Michael Peter said at her shoulder.

Sister Joan would've leapt out of her skin if she hadn't frozen with shock. For an instant she was incapable of speech or movement. Then she managed to swallow, to step aside slightly as she replied, 'It's most effective. I'm sure the visitors will be impressed.'

'All the costumes are authentic,' he said.

'Yes. Yes, you mentioned it. The figures—?'

'I bought the entire contents of an old waxworks show. The owners were going bankrupt, so I was able to obtain them very cheaply. They look quite effective, don't you think?'

'Very,' Sister Joan said.

'I hate to hurry you but a dealer has arrived so I'm going to have to talk to him,' he said. 'I brought the chalice and all the relevant receipts and papers. You can leave by the back. Of course, I shall turn that into the official visitors' entrance when I formally open the exhibition. But you haven't had sufficient time to appreciate everything! Look, this is a spare key. If you turn it twice in the back door it will deactivate the alarm system in this part of the building and open the door at the same time. I know you'll be careful and lock up again when you leave. They like to be visited, you know.'

He put the key in her hand along with the large carrier bag in which the cardboard box reposed, gave his odd, skeletal smile and went away.

The phrase hung in her mind. They like to be visited. Was that what Michael Peter did? Night after night when he'd driven Mrs Rufus home did he slip in here, to cherish his heartless, lifeless family? It was an unnerving idea and she went quickly down the back stairs and unlocked the door at the bottom. At least if visitors were going to enter that way they would see the funeral scene first and progress backwards through the imagined lives of people who had never lived.

Outside in the narrow entry she drew a long deep breath of fresh air, and turned to walk back to the main street.

Sister Jerome who ruled her priestly charges like a strict boarding-school matron opened the door to her, her grim face relaxing into what was the nearest she ever came to a smile. The impression she gave the world was the mask she wore to hide a life too filled with past pain and remorse.[1] Sister Joan never met her without feeling intense gratitude that her own existence had been so sunny.

'The fathers are out,' Sister Jerome said by way of greeting.

'Yes, I hoped they would be. Has Father Stephens mentioned the gift for Father Malone?'

'He has indeed,' Sister Jerome said. 'Father Stephens may be a man of the cloth but he has the sense to ask my advice. Did you obtain a chalice?'

'I have it here. I was going to take it back to the convent and keep it there but it occurred to me that it might be better concealed on the spot.'

'I'll keep it hidden,' Sister Jerome said, taking the carrier bag and giving it a look that warned it not to allow its contents to escape. 'You'll have a cup of tea, Sister Joan.'

It was a statement, not a question but Sister Joan said meekly, 'Yes, thank you, Sister.'

'I'll put the kettle on.'

She led the way into the spotless kitchen.

'I bought it at Michael Peter's antique shop,' Sister Joan said, taking the seat offered to her.

'That's an expensive place, isn't it?' Sister Jerome looked at her.

'Very,' Sister Joan said, 'but for some reason Mr Peter agreed to sell a chalice to me for far less than its market price. I can't think why.'

'Bowled over by your charm probably,' Sister Jerome said dryly, getting out mugs.

'Oh, I do hope not,' Sister Joan said fervently.

The idea of bowling Michael Peter over with charm or anything else struck her as an intensely unpleasant notion.

'You don't like him?'

'He's been very polite to me, very helpful,' Sister Joan said, 'and he's clearly very good at his job. But there's something –

[1] See *Vow of Penance*

no, I can't say that I like him very much.'

'I've looked in the windows once or twice,' Sister Jerome said, pouring the tea. 'Not that I've much time to go staring in shop windows. The fathers are like a pair of children when it comes to putting socks in the wash or taking their vitamins. Now and then though I do have a look,' Sister Jerome said. 'There are some lovely things there. Too valuable for most people.'

'I think he trades mainly with dealers. He's married you know.'

'Is he? I've never seen any wife,' Sister Jerome said. 'Help yourself to milk and sugar, Sister. The biscuits are almond ones, freshly made. You'll not offend me by refusing one.'

'Thank you. I wasn't going to refuse,' Sister Joan said. 'Your almond biscuits are like manna from heaven.'

'They're biscuits, not biscuits from any miraculous source,' Sister Jerome said with a pleased scowl. 'I'll give you some to take back to the convent for the rest of the community. So Mr Peter is married! I heard somwhere that he had a full-time housekeeper.'

'Mrs Rufus. Do you know her?'

'Never laid eyes on her,' Sister Jerome said. 'What's your interest in her?'

'She's gone to Torquay for the day,' Sister Joan said thoughtfully.

'They tell me that it's a very nice place. Bracing.'

'She didn't mention it to me.'

'Oh, you know her then?' Sister Jerome sipped her tea.

'Only slightly. I went to Mr Peter's house to telephone the police after I found that poor man dead in the old chapel.'

'I heard about that.'

'It didn't get into the newspapers, did it?'

'No, it was Father Malone mentioned it.' Sister Jerome gave her a severe look. 'If you want my honest opinion, Sister, this finding dead bodies is a bad habit. Not that I suppose you do it deliberately. Some women attract boyfriends; other women attract money; you attract dead bodies, I daresay.'

'Thank you,' Sister Joan said sweetly.

'I always speak my mind. You know that, Sister. Well, I'd best get this hidden. Do you have the receipt for it?'

'Everything's in the carrier bag,' Sister Joan said, finishing her tea.

'Good. I like to be careful with things. Nowadays people live in a throw-away world and don't take care of things they own. Easy come, easy go! Constable Brown was telling me earlier – he pops in for a cup of tea from time to time – that only this morning a large suitcase crammed with very good clothes was handed in at the station. Someone found it on the embankment. Would you believe it?'

'Yes,' Sister Joan said, watching the other fill a small tin with the almond crescents.

'Give my best wishes to the rest of the community.'

Sister Jerome was showing her out. Sister Joan, her head full of discarded clothes, gave her an absentminded God bless! and walked on down the street.

At the police station she was relieved to find no sign of Constable Brown. Only a young trainee officer manned the desk, springing smartly to attention as she came in.

'Yes, Sister! How may I help you?' He sounded eager for promotion already.

'I understand a suitcase full of clothes was found on the embankment,' she said.

'It was brought in early this morning,' the constable said. 'They aren't nuns' clothes, Sister.'

'I wondered if I might have a look at them,' Sister Joan said. 'It's always possible that I might recognize something that someone I know has worn.'

'I suppose it won't do any harm. They're in the back office.'

He lifted the flap of the counter and came round to escort her through to the back premises where the suitcase stood, neatly labelled Lost Property, in a corner.

'They're very expensive clothes, Sister.' He lifted the suitcase, laid it on the side table, and unclasped the lid. 'Very good taste. My girlfriend would give her eyeteeth for some of these. I've said to her, "Now, Brenda, why keep fretting about the way you're dressed? Me, I like you better with nothing on at a—" ' His voice trailed away and he stared at her in embarrassed horror.

'Of course you do,' Sister Joan said. 'I'll bet she's smashing. Ah, these are very expensive, aren't they?'

'Real silk,' the constable said, recovering his composure slightly. 'Look, sable cuffs on this suit. Not that I think it's right to wear fur, mind, but it does lift a jacket out of the ordinary, doesn't it?'

'Certainly it does.' She watched as he carefully lifted some of the garments for her inspection.

They were size twelve, she estimated, designed for someone a couple of inches taller than herself. Their pastel shades with blue predominating suggested they were more suited to a blonde than a brunette. At the bottom of the suitcase, neatly folded, was underwear, silk slips and French knickers and several pairs of filmy tights that looked unworn.

'Thank you, Constable. You've been very helpful,' she said.

'To tell you the truth, Sister.' He was replacing the various items carefully. 'To tell you the truth I'm not sure I was authorized to show them, but as it's a religious lady—'

'Perhaps it would be wiser not to mention it to Constable Brown?'

'I think you're right, Sister. Thank you.'

As he showed her out he asked hopefully, 'I don't suppose you recognized any of the clothes, did you?'

'I didn't recognize any of the garments at all,' Sister Joan said. That at least was true, she thought, as she hurried back to the van.

EIGHT

Slowing and stopping as she reached the schoolhouse, she was gripped by mixed emotions when she saw Caroline standing, peering nervously out of the open door. After a couple of days of not seeing her she was struck afresh by the other's tense, miserable look, hands clutching the baggy brown sweater, hair pulled back into a lank ponytail. One couldn't help feeling pity for the girl and wanting to help her, but at the same time one couldn't help wondering what made her so spineless. In Caroline's place Sister Joan would've marched boldly up to Michael Peter's front door and demanded to know the whereabouts of her sister.

'I was afraid you might have forgotten me,' Caroline said, opening the door wider and standing aside.

'I thought it might do you some good to rest up for a little while,' Sister Joan said, 'and anyway I've been busy.'

'Have you found Crystal?' A trace of eagerness had come into Caroline's mild eyes.

'N – not exactly. No, I haven't found her,' Sister Joan said slowly, sitting down on one of the hard chairs. 'Look, I have found out something but I don't think that it's something you're going to want to hear.'

'What is it?' Caroline who had also seated herself sat bolt upright.

'Some days ago I found the body of a man in the abandoned chapel near the Peter house,' Sister Joan said. 'I think it was your father.'

'Dad?' Caroline stared at her. 'That's not possible! Dad's in the Heart Unit having further tests and treatment and he thinks that I'm staying with friends.'

'I rang the hospital and he hadn't turned up for his appointment.'

'You mean he came down into Cornwall? Without telling me?'

'He was worried about your sister too, wasn't he?' Sister Joan said.

'We were both anxious,' Caroline said. 'We could never get a proper answer on the telephone and no letters were coming. I never told Dad about her sending me the gold initial. He didn't know about our arrangement anyway. It was a private one, made in a spirit of fun. Dad can't stand too much stress, not with his heart the way it is.'

'The man who died in the chapel had an enlarged heart,' Sister Joan said. 'He died of a heart attack.'

'But why wasn't I informed? Why didn't somebody come and tell me?' Caroline demanded. 'Oh, of course, I was already down here by then. They'll be sending out radio messages or something.'

'They don't know yet who the man was,' Sister Joan said. 'He had no identification on him.'

'You mean he was robbed?'

'I think that he got rid of them,' Sister Joan said, 'or, to be exact, I thought that in the beginning but now I think that the items were removed so as to make any identification difficult. Caroline, do you recognize these?'

She brought out the credit card, pen and watch from the depths of her pocket.

'That's Dad's pen,' Caroline said. 'I bought it for him last Christmas. The watch too. Crystal and I got him that about three years back. There's an inscription on the inside of the back. I don't understand. Where did you get them?'

'They were hidden in the shower room at Michael Peter's house.'

'I knew it!' Spurred by sudden animation Caroline sprang to her feet and began to pace restlessly up and down. 'I knew that Michael Peter was evil. I sensed it. Crystal was never very clever where men were concerned. But I sensed it when they never asked us to the wedding. Now why would they do that unless she was afraid that I'd see what he was really like? If they were in his house then he killed Dad.'

'The death was due to a heart attack. He probably set out to walk to the house and went into the chapel to rest either on the way there or the way back.'

'But you found his things in the house!'

'Which doesn't prove who hid them there,' Sister Joan said patiently. 'And it wasn't murder.'

'But if the things were in the house – can't Michael Peter be arrested?'

'I daresay the police might want to ask him a few questions,' Sister Joan said, 'but he could simply deny any knowledge of their existence.'

'And after that he'd really be on his guard,' Caroline said slowly, sitting down again.

'I'm sorry.' Sister Joan looked at her sympathetically. 'I'm not handling this for you very well, but I did warn you that I wasn't a professional. I'm not even a very good amateur detective! I just stumble into situations now and then and sometimes I find the right way out again. I know you don't want to go back to the police but they would have to take you more seriously this time.'

'But it would alert Michael Peter,' Caroline said.

'I reckon that if anything has happened to your sister he'll be alerted already. Caroline, did your sister ever wear a jacket with sable cuffs?'

'Michael Peter bought her a skirt and jacket,' Caroline said slowly. 'The jacket had sable cuffs. She mentioned it in one of the letters she sent. I remembered that Dad laughed and said he'd always dreamed of seeing one of us wrapped in mink but sables would do at a pinch.'

'Can you describe any other clothes she wore?'

'She didn't come round every week to see us even before she went off and got married,' Caroline said, knuckling her cheek pensively. 'She loved pastel shades. Her being so fair they flattered her colouring. And she adored lacy undies – real silk and a bit sexy.'

'And you don't know exactly where she worked?'

'She liked to change jobs fairly often so as not to get into a rut,' Caroline said. 'Of course for most people it isn't so easy to do that nowadays with unemployment so high but she was so pretty and charming that she could talk her way into anything she fancied. She did some escort work for various agencies and she had a couple of jobs as receptionist. If she'd been taller she could've been a model. She had a lovely figure. Why am I talking about her as if she's dead? I don't want her to be dead, Sister! If she's gone and I've lost Dad, then there isn't anybody.'

'I'm sorry.' Sister Joan shook her head slightly. 'I'm truly sorry, but there isn't anything anyone can say. Not at a time like this! Look, if you want to go to the police I'll take you there and tell them my part in all this. There doesn't seem to be much further we can go by ourselves.'

'Why did you ask me about Crystal's clothes?' Caroline asked.

'A large suitcase crammed with rather expensive garments was found on the embankment. It had been thrown from a train probably. The other day I saw Mr Peter on his way to catch a train to London, for a business meeting he said. He was carrying a large suitcase. Today I made an excuse to call in at the police station and saw the same suitcase in the back office there.'

'And the clothes were like the ones that Crystal would wear?'

'I'm sorry.' Sister Joan rose. 'Look, if those clothes could be identified as having belonged to your sister, and I made a statement about having found your father's things in the bathroom at the house, the police would certainly launch an immediate enquiry. I know you think that Michael Peter would be put on the alert and start covering his tracks but Crystal hasn't communicated with you since Easter. Don't you think he'll have covered up his tracks already and the longer time goes on the more difficult it's going to be to get any evidence at all?'

'Do you really want to know the truth?' Caroline had risen again and walked to the door. 'Sister, I'm scared! I'm scared of finding out what really happened to Crystal. I know it's stupid and I know that I can't change anything if it has happened, but I keep on hoping that she'll suddenly turn up, just walk in and explain everything. We were always so close that I honestly don't know what I'd do if—'

'You'd survive,' Sister Joan said. 'Honestly you would. Look, let's leave it until tomorrow. Sleep on it and I'll come by tomorrow. By then I'm hoping to have put a bit more of the jigsaw together. How are the supplies lasting out? I should've brought you some more.'

'I don't eat very much at the best of times,' Caroline said. 'I'm fine, Sister. Honestly, I'm fine.'

'Tomorrow then.' Sister Joan spoke as cheerfully as she could, aware that nothing she said sounded adequate. 'I'll bring you something for lunch tomorrow and then we could both go down and talk to the police.'

'Thank you, Sister.'

The door closed behind her and she heard the key turn in the lock. It had been, she reflected, getting back into the van, a thoroughly unsatisfactory interview. The problem was that Caroline Hayes was obviously in shock, having nerved herself to travel into Cornwall she was now unable to take action, terrified of what she might learn, scared of Michael Peter's discovering her presence in the neighbourhood.

Going in through the kitchen door of the convent she almost bumped into Sister Perpetua who raised sandy brows and remarked snappishly, 'How is it that you're never here when you're needed, Sister Joan?'

'Am I needed? I went on an errand for Reverend Mother,' Sister Joan said in surprise.

'I needed several things in town but you didn't wait around long enough to find out!'

'Sister, I'm truly sorry! Mother Dorothy was keen for me to get off early. Do you want me to drive in after lunch? It wouldn't be any trouble,' Sister Joan said.

'I daresay it wouldn't.' Sister Perpetua refused to be mollified. 'It never is any trouble to you to go dashing off out of the enclosure on the slightest pretext!'

'Then you take the van. I'm sure Mother Dorothy wouldn't

refuse permission.' A decided sparkle had come into Sister Joan's blue eyes.

'We're not all as fond of gallivanting as you are, Sister!'

'If you write down what you need I'll drive down and get it.'

There were times, Sister Joan thought, keeping the smile on her face with an effort when it was difficult to feel sisterly love and kindness twenty-four hours a day.

'I've made a list.'

'Fine! then I'll drive down into town and get them, or would you like me to miss lunch and gallop in right this minute?'

Sister Perpetua stared at her for a moment, then unexpectedly grinned. 'I'm sorry, Sister,' she said. 'I got out of the wrong side of the bed this morning, and I've snapped everybody's head off! Don't take it personally. The fact is that Sister Mary Concepta had a bit of a heart spasm during the night and I spent a couple of hours sitting with her. After that it was hard to get back to sleep.'

'You should've called somebody,' Sister Joan said.

'Oh, it wasn't a serious attack but the poor soul gets frightened.'

'Might it not be a good idea to call in the doctor?' Sister Joan ventured. It was always a risk to mention the medical profession to Sister Perpetua who considered her own herbal remedies as far more efficacious.

'It might not hurt,' Sister Perpetua said unwillingly. 'Tell him there's no hurry but it would relieve Sister Mary Concepta's mind. We'd better go to lunch.'

Looking marginally less irritable, she plodded ahead up the stairs.

Luncheon over, Sister Joan collected a list of items required by the infirmarian, got the requisite permission to go back into town from Mother Dorothy, and slipped into the infirmary where Sister Mary Concepta, retaining the flowerlike blue eyes of her girlhood in a delicate, old-lady face, sat with a rug over her knees by the fire.

'Are you all right, Sister?' Sister Joan looked at the fragile figure anxiously.

At eighty-two the older nun had one of the sweetest natures

in the community. Her ill health had become something that
people took for granted, but the possibility that she might be
deteriorating suddenly occurred to Sister Joan.

'Oh, I'm much better this afternoon,' Sister Mary Concepta
said. 'Has Sister Perpetua been frightening the life out of you? I
had a nasty little turn during the night, that's all. After all I am
eighty-two, you know.'

'I'm five years older than you are,' Sister Gabrielle said,
coming in, 'and I don't make near as much fuss about it as you
do.'

'You've always enjoyed excellent health,' Sister Mary
Concepta said. 'Not all of us are so blessed.'

'Nonsense! You've a vivid imagination, that's all.' Sister
Gabrielle tapped her way to the fireside and lowered herself
heavily into her chair. 'If you're thinking of asking the doctor to
call in then you'd better tell him to check me over at the same
time, because my rheumatism has been playing up a lot,
though I don't complain about it.'

'I hope you're not suggesting that I'm in the habit of
grumbling, Sister?' Sister Mary Concepta's face was gently
reproving.

'If the cap fits—' Sister Gabrielle tapped her stick on the floor
and looked at Sister Joan. 'If you're going, child, you'd best
make tracks,' she said. 'We're neither of us spring chickens!'

She left them to their amiable squabbling and went out to the
van. She'd call in at the doctor's and arrange for him to visit
Sisters Mary Concepta and Gabrielle. Get the things Sister
Perpetua wanted. Buy some supplies for Caroline Hayes. Go
and see if Mrs Rufus had really gone to Torquay.

That last instruction wrote itself unexpectedly on her mind
as she drove down the track into the main street. It was
ridiculous, of course. Mrs Rufus had gone to Torquay for the
whole day. She wouldn't be back until the evening at the
earliest.

The local doctor had retired the previous year and his
shabby, reassuring waiting-room was now a coldly clinical
place with glass separating the receptionist from the patients,
either to avoid infection or to prevent them stealing the medical

forms – she wasn't sure which, hard chairs, and notices ordering people never to smoke, never to drink, never to indulge in unsafe sex. Such notices always made her feel an urge to light up, down a quick whisky and grab the nearest man.

'Sister Mary Concepta?' The receptionist tapped a number in on the small computer that stood on the counter and studied the screen. 'She was visited six months ago by Doctor Elroyd. Dr Flecker is free tomorrow if it's a home visit she requires. We do prefer patients to come to the surgery whenever possible.'

'Sister Mary Concepta is in her eighties and hasn't left the enclosure for years,' Sister Joan said. 'Isn't it possible for Dr Elroyd to visit? She's used to him.'

'A non-urgent case, is it?' The receptionist consulted her mechanical toy again and smiled graciously. 'Ten o'clock on Friday morning. Of course if her condition worsens before then do inform us. Thank you.'

Sister Joan thanked her back and left with the feeling that patients were no longer regarded as people but as units to be moved about on some vast appointments board. When the individual was pushed aside then what price was self-adoration then? It might make an interesting subject for discussion.

She walked on to the chemist and piled Sister Perpetua's requirements into a wire basket, noting with amusement that a packet of henna was on the list. Sister Perpetua was battling valiantly against the grey!

Coffee, tea, milk, bread and some fresh cheese would keep Caroline Hayes fairly well supplied for a day or two. Her purchases made, she dumped them in the van, and told herself firmly that there was no reason whatsoever for her to drive round to the house where Michael Peter had told her Mrs Rufus lived.

Instead she crossed the road to the florist's and spent some of her own vastly diminished pocket money on a small bunch of flowers. It seemed so wrong that John Hayes should have become in death no more than another statistic. She doubted if Caroline would've had the idea of coming to the cemetery to find her father's grave. Caroline's mind was fixed firmly on her missing sister, and she'd scarcely seemed to register the fact that her father had died.

Sister Joan got back into the van and drove up towards the new cemetery on the edge of the housing estate. The old cemetery was protected historic property now, but all burials were in the new ground near the ugly, red-roofed villa which had replaced the old vicarage.

She parked the van at the gates and set off briskly along the gravelled path. All the headstones here were less than twenty years old, with the epitaphs on them strictly conforming to good taste and large monuments discouraged. No doubt there was a computer somewhere with lists of the corpses on it, she thought, and stopped in her tracks, staring at the yellow tape that was stretched in a square around the grave of the man who had almost certainly been Caroline and Crystal's father. Part of the space within the tape was occupied by a tarpaulin with the sides hiding whatever – whoever? lay within.

A tall, good-looking man, black hair lightly winged with silver, ducked out from beneath the tarpaulin and stood for a moment looking at her before he strode forward.

'I had a feeling that someone was missing from the scene!' he exclaimed. 'How are you, Sister Joan?'

'Detective Sergeant Mill!' Her pleasure beamed out spontaneously. 'I thought you were on holiday.'

'There's a limit to the amount of holiday that I can endure,' he said wryly. 'Are those flowers meant for this grave?'

'They were,' Sister Joan said. 'I was the one who found the body.'

'So Constable Brown told me with great disapproval. Wait a moment, Sister.' He went back beneath the tarpaulin for a moment, re-emerged and stepped over the tape. 'I'm not required here for the moment. The photographer's just finishing up and then we'll move her to the path. lab.'

'Her?' Sister Joan looked at him as they began to walk slowly along the path.

'Her name's Mary Rufus. She lived over on the new estate. Widow.'

'So she didn't go to Torquay,' Sister Joan said.

'You know her?'

'We met. She housekept for Michael Peter, the antique dealer.'

'Tall, grey-haired chap. Looks like Don Quixote. I suppose you know him too?'

'Only slightly. Alan, what happened?'

'A lady came to put flowers on a relative's grave and found Mrs Rufus lying on the new grave. The back of her head had been stoved in. Very nasty. There were some flowers scattered round her. Did she have any connection with the body you found?'

'I went to Michael Peter's house to ring the police after I found him,' Sister Joan said. 'She was a nice woman. Grim on the outside but kind-hearted within. I suppose she felt sorry for the dead man and decided to put some flowers on his grave. That's why I'm here myself.'

'Give the flowers to me. I'll see they're put on the grave.' He took the blooms, his expression poised between curiosity and affectionate amusement. 'What's all this about Torquay?'

'Michael Peter told me that she was going there for the day.'

'So either she changed her mind but took the day off anyway or she gave him an excuse that wasn't true in the beginning or—'

'Or Michael Peter lied.'

'Why would he do that?'

'I don't know yet,' Sister Joan said.

'We haven't found the murder weapon yet.'

'If it crushed her skull it must've been very heavy.' Sister Joan crossed herself, thinking of Mrs Rufus who had been grumpy but kind-hearted and who had craved a bit of company during the long hours in the lonely house.

'Or the killer was very strong and very determined,' Detective Sergeant Mill said. 'What's your interest in all this, Sister?'

'It's a long story and I'm due back at the convent.'

'And I've got to finish up here before I start interviewing people and taking statements. Have you anything to tell me that can't wait until tomorrow?'

'I don't think so,' she said uncertainly.

'Right then! Can you come down to the station first thing tomorrow? We'll have a long chat then.'

'I'll be there at nine,' she promised.

'I've had Sergeant Brown wished on me. Excellent officer.' He looked gloomy. 'It seems Petrie has the measles! How are they all up at the convent? How are you, Sister?'

'We're all much the same. Sister Mary Concepta is a bit frailer but the doctor's coming on Friday to check her over.' When Alan Mill asked after people he genuinely wanted to know. It was a facet of his personality she found particularly pleasing.

'And you? Would I be right in guessing that something's going on?'

'Something I can't fathom,' she said frankly. 'I'm awfully glad you're back.'

'Yes.' His dark eyes rested briefly on her face. 'Yes, I'm glad to be back myself. You accused me once of being a workaholic. That's not strictly true. I find myself looking at my job as a kind of respite from holiday periods.'

'I'm sorry you didn't enjoy yourself.'

'Actually I did. The boys are growing up fast though and they don't really want dear old Dad trailing after them and cramping their style. My wife worries about them.'

'Very natural surely?'

'I suppose.' He made a little grimace, then seemed to shake it off. 'Sister, I'd better get back and give a few final instructions re the mopping-up operations. You'll be at the station tomorrow?'

'Tomorrow.'

Climbing up into the van she felt a surge of optimism. Now that Detective Sergeant Mill was back life seemed brighter. It only meant, of course, that she now had a sympathetic ally in the Force.

'One more thing!' He put his hand on the half-open window.

'Yes?'

'You weren't surprised when you heard that Mary Rufus had been killed.'

'I think that I was expecting it,' Sister Joan said, and let in the clutch.

Before she made her statement she needed to talk to Caroline. It was too late now to hold back, to try to discover more. This second death was no accident. Caroline must come with her to see Detective Sergeant Mill.

The door of the schoolhouse was ajar. Sister Joan took out the bag of groceries she'd bought and swung herself down from the van, calling as she approached the door, 'It's only me – Sister Joan! Are you there?'

There was no reply and when she pushed the door wider she walked into an empty building. Empty but not untenanted, she thought, looking round and seeing the half-finished cup of cold tea on the table, the blankets tossed on the narrow bunk bed, the cold water with a scum of soap on it in one of the washbasins.

'Caroline? Caroline!'

She raised her voice, knowing there was nobody there.

The girl had probably plucked up her courage and decided to go out after all. It was just bad luck that she'd chosen this particular time. Sister Joan frowned as she went outside again and looked round.

Nothing moved in the light spring breeze except the tall grasses that waved sunglinted spears beyond the shorter turf that bordered the stony track that led in one direction into the town and in the other to the convent. At the side of the building the old car in which Brother Cuthbert loved to tinker while his mind was on higher matters stood, fenders rusting, the boot wedged slightly open.

She found herself walking towards the car, each step slow and unwilling. There was a dry taste in her mouth as she leaned down and released the piece of wood that held the door of the boot ajar, then stepped back as it sprang upwards to reveal a small pile of clothes.

They were familiar these garments: a shapeless brown sweater and a matching skirt with the hem ripped away from its stitching now, and the smell of drying blood on both garments. She put out her hand and touched the stiffly dried wool. The skirt and the sweater were here, but there was no Caroline. There was no Caroline at all.

NINE

'Sit down, take a deep breath and tell me what's happened.' Detective Sergeant Mill nodded to the chair at the side of his desk. 'Do you want me to telephone the convent?'

'No – yes.' Sister Joan sat down. 'It won't matter if I'm a little late but Sister Perpetua was waiting for some things from the chemist. Perhaps I'd better—'

'Are they in the back of the van?'

'In a large carrier bag, yes.'

'Give me your keys. I'll have Constable Whitney take the stuff up to the convent and tell them you're likely to be late.'

'Constable Whitney?'

'Wished on me from Penzance while Petrie's *hors de combat*. Drink the tea.'

He took the keys and went out briskly. Sister Joan drank the tea shiveringly.

'You've had a shock.' Detective Sergeant Mill came back into the office and sat down. 'Not another body, I hope?'

'A torn skirt and a sweater with drying blood on them, in the boot of the old car at the side of the schoolhouse,' Sister Joan said. 'They belong – belonged to Caroline Hayes—'

'Who is?'

'The daughter of the man I found dead in the old chapel. She's renting the schoolhouse from us until – for a week or so. Brother Cuthbert went to Scotland.'

'Hold on a minute!'

He rose again and went out. She could hear voices in quick consultation.

'Constable Brown and the Special are on their way to cordon off the area,' he said, returning. 'You'd better bring me up to date as succinctly as possible.'

'I found the body in the old chapel when I was out exercising Lilith and I went to the nearest house, which happened to be Michael Peter's house, though I didn't know it then,' Sister Joan said. 'I phoned the police from there. The man had died of a heart attack and he had no identification on him.'

'That much I already know.'

'Caroline Hayes turned up to ask me for help. She'd read my name in that awful newspaper article and got the idea that I was some kind of private detective. She told me that she was worried about her sister Crystal. Crystal got married last year to Michael Peter and came to live in Cornwall, but neither Caroline nor her father had been asked to the wedding and though Crystal had written to them in the beginning she hadn't communicated since Easter. She'd sent an initial C, a piece of jewellery – Mr Hayes had given his daughters one each and they'd made a private arrangement to send the other the initial if they ever needed urgent help. Crystal had sent the initial just before Easter but Caroline and her father were moving house and the mail was delayed.'

'So she came down to Cornwall with her father?' He was making rapid notes.

'No, she didn't want to worry him because of his bad heart so she said she was going on holiday with friends while her father was receiving treatment in hospital. It seems that he decided to come down here independently to try and see Crystal and something happened. He didn't keep his appointment at the Heart Unit because I checked it out.'

'Go on.'

Sister Joan went on, rapidly recounting the visit she had paid to the Peter house, the finding of the watch, credit card and pen in the toilet roll—'

'Do you have them still?'

'They're here.' She took them out of her pocket and laid them on the desk. 'Oh, and I found this in the old chapel, scuffed under the earth. It looks as if he jotted down the name and telephone number.'

'You should've handed these in at the station.'

'I was going to do that but Constable Petrie wasn't here and you were on holiday and, quite frankly, I didn't have much confidence in the officers who were here. I found that strip of paper after the old chapel had been searched, and when Caroline Hayes came to the station to report her sister missing they didn't seem to take her seriously.'

'Had she been to the house or the antique shop to ask where her sister was?'

'She didn't want Michael Peter to know she was in the area. She thought it'd make him cover his tracks more thoroughly.'

'She sounds,' said Detective Sergeant Mill, with deep disapproval, 'like a most hysterical young woman. Why on earth leap to the conclusion that Michael Peter had any tracks to cover when she hadn't even been up to the house?'

'Because she'd received the initial I suppose. She's a very highly-strung kind of person, very nervy. She asked me to make a couple of enquiries on her behalf.'

'And?'

'Michael Peter told me that his wife was touring France with her family.'

'So this sister does exist.'

'There's a photograph of Crystal and Caroline in Michael Peter's house, and I sent off to St Catherine's House to get their birth certificates. Caroline mentioned where they were born and their star signs. I do try to check up, you know,' she said reproachfully.

'In the absence of an efficient local police force?' His grin was still disapproving. 'Anyway you've told me now. We'd better get up to the schoolhouse. You can tell me the rest on the way.'

'There isn't any "rest",' she protested, going through the door he held open.

'There's Mrs Rufus.'

'Yes.' Walking towards the police car, she bit her lip, remembering. 'She worked as housekeeper for Michael Peter. Full-time but she doesn't sleep in and she doesn't go up to the house on Sundays. Oh, she doesn't – didn't drive. Mr Peter picks her up in the morning, drops her at the house and goes on down to the shop. Then in the evening he picks her up again and runs her home. She mentioned his wife. Said she played pop music and painted her nails.'

'Sexual jealousy?' He nodded towards the seat belt.

'Hardly!' Sister Joan said, fastening it. 'Mrs Rufus was a respectable widow. She'd worked for Mr Peter and his mother before the old lady died. And Michael Peter just isn't the kind of man to inspire a sexual passion.'

'You'd be surprised,' Detective Sergeant Mill said, 'how many unsuitable people do inspire a sexual passion. And Crystal Hayes married him, didn't she?'

'For money? His business is very successful. Caroline told me that her sister worked for various escort agencies and as a conference hostess – I think that she may have been a … not exactly a prostitute but a good-time girl. Caroline was very loyal about her but that was the impression I got. Anyway Mrs Rufus told me that Crystal was on holiday with her family in France, but probably she was only repeating what Michael Peter had told her.'

'You mentioned Torquay.'

'Michael Peter told me that she was taking today off because she wanted a day in Torquay. He was obviously lying.'

'Not necessarily,' he said. 'She might've planned to go to Torquay and decided to take a few flowers to the cemetery first. Did she strike you as the kind of person who'd take flowers to the grave of an unknown man?'

'Hard rind, soft centre,' Sister Joan said.

'Neatly put.' He slowed the car as they neared the schoolhouse. 'Is there anything else you haven't told me?'

'A large suitcase full of very expensive women's clothes was found on the embankment. The young constable let me see them. Caroline Hayes told me they sounded like the kind of clothes that her sister liked to wear. A couple of days ago I met Michael Peter on his way to the station with a very big suitcase. He said he was going up to London on business. The suitcase I saw looked exactly like the one he'd been carrying. That's about it.'

'I think we'll be having a word with Mr Michael Peter,' Detective Sergeant Mill said, stopping the car.

'Alan.' Sister Joan touched his arm as he prepared to alight. 'I wasn't deliberately withholding evidence from the police. Everything was so nebulous, so indistinct. As far as I could see a crime hadn't even been committed then. I told Caroline that I believed the dead man was her father because I thought that would spur her to go to the police. It was evident that something was going on that required investigation. She told me that she would. I offered to go with her.'

'This was before Mrs Rufus's body was found?'

Sister Joan nodded.

'When I learned what had happened I drove straight to the schoolhouse. I was going to insist that she came down and spoke to you. Then I found the clothes.'

'Let's take a look.'

He came round to open the door for her.

The inevitable tape had already been stretched round the old car and Constable Brown was standing guard, his expression hardening into disapproval as he saw the newcomers.

'Sister Joan, take a good long look and tell me if this is what you found,' Detective Sergeant Mill instructed.

Ducking beneath the tape she approached the rusting vehicle.

'Yes. There was a piece of wood wedged in the door of the boot holding it open a couple of inches. I pulled it out and the boot sprang up. There's the piece of wood.'

'Plastic bag, Constable. Not that I expect any prints on it. Criminals never leave any these days.'

'You might find mine,' Sister Joan said. 'I wasn't wearing gloves.'

'That's because you don't go round committing crimes. Are those the clothes?'

'Yes.'

'As you found them?'

'Not exactly, no. I picked them up. I'm sorry but it was instinctive. They're the clothes Caroline Hayes was wearing the last time I saw her. The hem of the skirt has partly come down and there seems to be drying blood on both garments. I simply dropped them back into the boot, jumped back in the van and drove to the police station.'

'Did you knock at the door of the schoolhouse?'

'The door's open,' Constable Brown interposed.

'It was open when I arrived here,' Sister Joan said. 'I went first to the school – I don't know why we keep calling it that when it hasn't been used as a school for ages! – and the door was open. I called to Caroline to let her know that it was only me, but there wasn't any answer so I went in.'

'Can you describe the interior before we take another look inside?'

'There was a half-empty cup of tea on the table,' Sister Joan said. 'It was cold, and the blankets were just piled anyhow on the bed. I went into the cloakroom. One of the basins was half-full of cold soapy water. I touched the side of the cup to test for heat but not anything else. Oh, except the door. I pushed that wider.'

'Don't worry, we'll eliminate your prints. Come inside and tell me if it still looks as you saw it.'

Stepping inside, looking round, she shook her head. 'It all looks the same,' she said. 'I can't see that anything has changed.'

'The key's on the inside of the lock.'

'There's only the one key,' Sister Joan explained. 'Brother Cuthbert gave it to me for Mother Dorothy, and then when we rented the place to Caroline Hayes I gave her the key.'

'So Mother Dorothy met her?'

'Nobody met her,' Sister Joan said. 'Oh, she'd spent a couple of nights at a bed and breakfast near the station. I can give you the address. She was nervous about staying in town in case she bumped into Michael Peter.'

'But they'd never met.'

'He had a photograph of her and Crystal together. She'd seen him too. When she first arrived she walked over to his house, meaning to snoop round and see if there was any sign of Crystal. She saw him arriving home from work. It was dark and he didn't see her but she could see him by the light of the headlamps. She told me that he was grinning.'

'Grinning?'

'Smiling, but he has that long bony face and that wide thin mouth, and when he does smile it's more like a stretching of his facial muscles than anything else. You've seen him?'

'Once or twice. We're not personally acquainted. Constable Petrie went down to advise him on additional security for his premises and said he seemed a nice enough old cove.'

'He's forty-five.'

'Ah well, anyone over forty is in the running for a telegram from the Queen according to Petrie,' Detective Sergeant Mill said with a smile. 'What impression have you gained of him?'

'He's polite, very keen on the past as you might expect from an antique dealer. I'd guess that he ran an honest business and that he really cares about the things he sells. He talks a lot about his dear mother, Rose, whom he claims to have adored though I get the impression she was one of those suffocatingly sweet mothers who hang on like grim death to their bachelor sons. He waited nearly five years after her death before he married. He met Crystal Hayes at a trade fair.'

'Is this Caroline Hayes's bag?' He stooped to pull it from beneath the bed.

'A soft-topped suitcase, yes.'

'We'd better take a look.'

He lifted it to the table and unzipped it.

'Navy-blue sweater, blue T-shirt, pair of jeans, two pairs of socks, a pair of slippers, a pair of shortie pyjamas, both blue, a brown dressing-gown, some underwear in a plastic folder. Tissues. This is pretty.' He picked up the black embroidered lacy handkerchief.

'Crystal gave it to her. She was so nervous about actually asking for my help that she actually dropped it in chapel, hoping that I'd follow her.'

'Toothbrush, toothpaste, moisture cream, flannel and soap, a bath towel. That seems to be it. Ah, there's a pocket at the side.' His fingers dug within and emerged.

'That's the initial letter that Crystal sent her as a sign that she needed help,' Sister Joan said. 'It wasn't on its chain.'

'Looks like real gold.' He turned it over in his palm.

'John Hayes, their father, bought a gold initial for Crystal and a silver one for Caroline. She was wearing it beneath her sweater.'

'Her coat isn't here,' Detective Sergeant Mill said. 'Was she wearing a coat? It's still a bit chilly in the evenings.'

'A brown coat, straight cut and rather long. It was a bit shabby – but you saw it.'

'Saw what?'

'The coat. I mean Caroline Hayes in the coat. She went to the police station and told them her sister was missing.'

'She didn't tell me.'

'But she said—' Sister Joan closed her eyes, summoning memory. 'She said that she'd been down to the police station and spoken to a detective sergeant called Mill. Tall, dark and good-looking.'

'From which description you recognized me immediately. Thank you, Sister.'

'She mentioned the name Mill. I'm certain she did.'

'Then it'll be in the report book.'

'No, it isn't. I asked if she had been there making enquiries – I wanted to make sure she'd told me the truth. Constable Brown confirmed that he'd spoken to a Miss Hayes but hadn't put it in the book.'

'Someone tries to report a relative missing and he doesn't enter it in the book? What the devil is Brown playing at?'

He strode to the door, pulled it wide and summoned Constable Brown in a tone that boded ill.

'Sir?'

'Well, he's tall and dark,' Detective Sergeant Mill said with a faint grin. 'You haven't been passing yourself off as me in my absence, have you, Brown?'

'No, sir, not at any time,' Constable Brown said, looking more affronted than usual.

'But a Miss Hayes did come in making enquiries?'

'About her sister? Yes, sir. She asked for you but you weren't in the office. I dealt with the matter and she left.'

'You didn't enter it in the book?'

'Constable Petrie was duty officer that day,' Constable

Brown said with hauteur. 'It was for him to make entries.'

'I'll have a word with Petrie. Can you describe this Miss Hayes, Brown?'

'Thin, brown hair tied back, no make-up,' Constable Brown said. 'She was wearing a rather shabby brown coat. Very ladylike in her manner.'

'Thank you, Constable. We'd better get things cleared up here pretty quickly.'

'Thank you, sir.' Constable Brown darted a look at Sister Joan that conveyed his private opinions and departed.

'Good-looking, d'ye think?' Detective Sergeant Mill glanced at Sister Joan with a hint of mischief.

'Some ladies might think so,' she said demurely. 'Being a religious—'

'Your mind is on higher things. Don't scowl, Sister! A little teasing doesn't hurt anybody and you've had a pretty nasty shock today.'

'I'm getting accustomed to them,' she said wryly. 'Alan, what do you think happened here today?'

'Hazarding a guess,' he said slowly, looking round, 'Caroline Hayes unlocked the door and let someone in.'

'She wouldn't have done that,' Sister Joan objected promptly. 'She was scared of being seen by anybody.'

'Then she opened the door to someone she knew. Her sister?'

'Crystal? Yes, she'd have opened the door for Crystal but she came here to look for her so why—'

'Someone might've stood outside and pretended to be Crystal? Taken her off guard?'

'It's possible I suppose.'

'There's no chain on the door. She only had to turn the key and someone outside could have barged in. Is Caroline Hayes an athletic kind of woman?'

'Thin and a bit droopy,' Sister Joan said. 'She doesn't have much go in her.'

'So someone could have burst in and overpowered her?'

'Yes. Yes, I think so. There don't seem to be any signs of a struggle.'

'The bed looks untidy.'

'Yes, I did notice that,' Sister Joan said. 'When I came by before the blankets were all neatly folded. Caroline's a neat, schoolmarmish kind of person.'

'What's her job?'

'Shorthand typist. She temps.'

'And if the intruder had a knife? We'll get the forensic chaps in at once. If there was blood spilt here there'll be traces.'

'You think Caroline Hayes is dead, don't you?'

'I think there's a strong possibility.'

'Then it's my fault,' Sister Joan said. 'I ought to have insisted on going with her to the police at once. Instead I allowed her to talk me into waiting a day or two and I left her here.'

'She was a grown-up person,' he said firmly. 'She had the right to choose. You can take a little of the blame for not reporting finding John Hayes's property at the Peter house – you didn't break in?'

'Of course I didn't break in,' Sister Joan said indignantly. 'Michael Peter asked me to have a cup of tea with him, and I needed to visit the bathroom.'

'You and Michael Peter seem on remarkably cosy terms for two people who hardly know each other.'

'I went back to the old chapel to see if I could find any more clues, and he just happened to come along, that's all. I've been in his shop twice. The first time to ask in a roundabout way about his wife. He was pretty curt with me for which I can't blame him. Afterwards I had to go there on convent business.'

'Sister Hilaria won the lottery?'

'From your mouth to God's ear!' She grinned at him, feeling guilt lift. 'No, it's to do with a gift for Father Malone from Father Stephens. Anyway I bought what was wanted and then Mr Peter gave me a private tour of the costume exhibition.'

'What exactly did you buy?'

'A communion chalice. The one that Father Malone uses in church is only silver washed, and not very handsome. Michael Peter had a very handsome one he'd picked up at a church auction and he let me have it for seven hundred and fifty pounds.'

'You must've charmed him out of his socks. Come on. I'll drive you back to the convent.'

'But what happened here?' she protested. 'After the person unknown burst in?'

'There must've been some kind of struggle.' He looked about him frowningly. 'The blankets are untidy as you told me and outside in the boot of the car were the sweater and skirt – for some reason whoever it was stripped them off and bundled them there.'

'And propped the boot with a piece of wood so that somebody'd be bound to notice them?'

'Killers sometimes play games.' There was no amusement in his eyes.

'And Mrs Rufus? She must've been killed first.'

'When did you last speak to Caroline Hayes?'

'This morning. At about eleven forty-five, maybe a little after that. I told her that I suspected the dead man I found had been her father. She didn't seem to take it in properly. Shock, I suppose. Anyway I told her that we ought to inform the police as quickly as possible. She promised to do that.'

'But you didn't go to the police.'

'I was due back for lunch and she wanted more time anyway. I told you that I ought not to have listened to her.'

'Then you drove down again into town.'

'To buy some things Sister Perpetua needed from the chemist. I was about to drive back when I saw the florist's shop and I thought it might be a nice gesture to put a few flowers on the grave. The rest you know.'

'Right then.' He glanced at her as they left the schoolhouse and walked to the car. 'I'll run you back in my car and drive your van over tomorrow morning. We'll have to take your prints down at the station for the purposes of elimination. You know the routine.'

'Will you find Caroline Hayes?'

'Alive or dead,' he said grimly, buckling his seat belt. 'There are things here that don't add up, Sister. I'll be very interested to hear what Michael Peter has to say.'

'Are you going to arrest him?'

'Invite him in for questioning. Look, his wife's been missing since Easter, and she sent a signal for help to her sister. Mr Peter told you that his wife was on holiday in France which obviously isn't true, and if the suitcase found on the embankment is really his property then he'll have to explain why he was throwing his wife's clothes away. And you found the items belonging to his father-in-law in his bathroom. Add to that the fact that his housekeeper has been found in the cemetery with the back of her head stove in and that his sister-in-law has disappeared under decidedly odd and suspicious circumstances and, to put it mildly, he's got a hell of a lot of explaining to do.'

'Don't swear,' she said automatically.

'You want to be in on the questioning? It can be arranged.'

'I'd much prefer it if you kept my name out of it,' she said promptly. 'You don't have to tell him who found the items in the bathroom, do you?'

'I'm applying for a search warrant the minute I'm back in town. I'll let you know if anything happens before tomorrow morning.'

'No, save it until tomorrow,' she said quickly. 'I'm a nun first and last, and anything else has to come a very long way behind. You can drop me here. There's Sister Martha coming.'

'See you tomorrow then.' Letting her out he said, the teasing back in his eyes, 'You're not sorry that I'm back, are you, Sister?'

'Of course not. I shall be very happy to see Constable Petrie back at his post too,' she answered demurely, and went to meet Sister Martha, hearing the grinding of gears as he turned and drove away again.

TEN

'I understand that Detective Sergeant Mill has returned early from his holiday,' Mother Dorothy said.

'Yes, Mother Prioress. Apparently he got bored.'

'A pity,' Mother Dorothy gave a little cough. 'A hardworking police officer ought to allow himself sufficient time to unwind, to strengthen the links with his family. You know, Sister, we religious are very fortunate. Our vocation gives us such joy that we never need to take a rest from worship even when we are engaged in the most mundane of tasks. Is there anything you wish to talk to me about?'

'I don't think so, Mother Dorothy. Oh, I am expecting a letter from St Catherine's House. Hopefully it will arrive tomorrow morning. May I have it as soon as it comes?'

All save urgent letters were distributed on Saturday mornings, having by then been read and if necessary censored by the prioress. Sister Katherine, in a rare moment of humour, had once observed, 'I don't expect ever to be elected prioress but if I am then it must be great to get to read all the letters before they have "applepie" scrawled over the interesting bits!'

'I take it that this letter is connected with the unfortunate man who died in the old chapel?'

'Yes, Mother Dorothy.'

'The young officer who so kindly brought the items that Sister Perpetua had ordered spoke of a body being found.'

'Mrs Rufus,' Sister Joan said. 'She was found in the cemetery with her skull fractured. She was Mr Peter's housekeeper—'

'And kindly allowed you to telephone from the house after

your discovery. May her soul and the souls of all the faithful departed rest in peace.'

'Amen,' Sister Joan said.

'I will hand the letter to you immediately it arrives,' Mother Dorothy said. 'Is our van to be returned soon?'

'Detective Sergeant Mill is bringing it back in the morning, Mother. I will have to drive it back down to town in order to have my fingerprints taken.'

'For purposes of elimination, I trust?' Mother Dorothy raised an eyebrow.

'Yes, of course!'

'If I were you, Sister,' Mother Dorothy said, 'I'd leave a set of my fingerprints permanently down at the station. It would save the inconvenience in the future.'

'I think that's against the law,' Sister Joan said.

'Happily we are constrained by a higher law. We had an excellent discussion this afternoon on the corrupting influence of adoration bestowed in the wrong place. Sister David very kindly took notes for you. Was there anything else?'

'May I miss recreation and spend the time in chapel?' Sister Joan asked. 'I need to catch up on my devotions.'

'But not at the expense of your sisters,' Mother Dorothy said. 'They would greatly miss the lively tone you bring to recreation, Sister. If you wish to pray you may remain behind in chapel after the final blessing for two hours.'

'Thank you, Mother Prioress.'

It was more than she had hoped. Worship was like food, she thought, as she joined the line mounting the staircase. Too much satiated the mind; too little left a gnawing emptiness.

Making the customary small announcements just before chapel ended, Mother Dorothy said, 'Certain rumours regarding local events may or may not have reached you. There has been a murder in the village. I tell you this so that you may remember the victim, Mary Rufus, in your prayers. Sister Joan has been excused community duties for a few days as she is helping the police in their enquiries, but she has requested extra time for her religious observances. I have therefore granted her leave to remain behind in chapel after the grand silence has begun, which makes her responsible for locking the inner door. Thank you, Sisters.'

One or two glances, amused, faintly critical, were cast in Sister Joan's direction before eyes were lowered again and the first decade of the glorious mysteries intoned.

When she knelt to receive the Blessing she gave her superior a fleeting smile of gratitude. Mother Dorothy had a way of smoothing one's path which contrasted with her crisp efficiency, or perhaps was part of it.

She rose and stood aside as Mother Dorothy turned to leave and Sister David moved to extinguish the candles on the altar. A moment more and silence reigned. Only the sanctuary lamp glowed redly in the dark and not even the early summer wind beyond the walls penetrated the calm. Sister Joan moved back to her accustomed place and knelt, forcing worldly matters out of her consciousness. She would ask for some enlightenment, she decided, for a way forward to be shown her so that this messy affair could speedily be resolved and she could return to her real task.

Enlightenment didn't come. Instead images whirled in her mind. The sickly sweet scent emanating from the body of John Hayes, the skeletal grin of Michael Peter, the wide, bewildered gaze of Caroline Hayes, the gruff kindliness of Mrs Rufus. Where were the two sisters now? Crystal and Caroline. Caroline and Crystal. Michael Peter must have fallen hard for a much younger woman in order to abandon his long bachelorhood and take a wife. And Crystal? Had she heard the chink of gold coins and decided to take what was on offer or had she felt something for the middle-aged man she'd married? The problem was that people presented only their outer personalities to others. It was too risky to appear naked and unadorned before humankind.

One person had died of natural causes; another had been murdered; two had vanished. She jerked her head up, willing away sleep.

Outside in the corridor a soft padding sound broke into her thoughts. She rose from her knees, sat for a moment, listening, then slid noiselessly from her place. The door into the corridor from the chapel was edged with baize to prevent its opening and closing from disturbing devotions. She opened it sufficiently wide to look out into the passage with its dim bulb glowing overhead. The padding became a scampering, and a furry shape leapt at her.

'Alice!' Inadvertently breaking the grand silence Sister Joan regained her balance and shook her head at the miscreant who immediately dropped to her haunches looking contrite.

Alice had no business here. She was supposed to be in her basket in the kitchen. Presumably she'd sensed someone in the chapel and come along to investigate, a sign, Sister Joan hoped, that she might have begun to take her role as guard dog more seriously. For a moment more she hesitated and then, moved by an impulse of which she was certain she would later be ashamed, she went to the outer door and drew the bolt.

'Go to bed!' She mouthed the words at Alice and went back into the chapel. For the next hour at least she was secure in the knowledge that nobody could get in from the outside.

It was past midnight when she returned to full consciousness of the material world. No great insights had come but she felt more resolute, more clearheaded. She drew back the bolt on the outer door, went through to the main hall and secured the connecting door, looking about her but seeing no sign of the dog. Presumably Alice had gone back to the kitchen. Sister Joan went across to the kitchen wing, trod softly past the infirmary and saw Alice, a dark bulk, curled demurely in her basket. Everything was as it should be within and the problems of the outside world could keep until morning. She moved to twitch the kitchen blind into place and froze, her hand without motion on the edge of the blind, her heart suddenly racing.

Outside in the yard a tall, cadaverous figure paced slowly across her line of vision and was lost to view. Michael Peter had chosen an unexpected area in which to take a late night walk.

She let the blind drop, drew a couple of deep breaths to steady her nerves and went softly to her cell.

'There is a letter for you from St Catherine's House,' Mother Dorothy delayed her after breakfast to tell her. 'It isn't personal?'

'No, Mother Prioress.'

'You may have it unopened.'

The manilla envelope was put into her hand. Sister Joan took it into the antechamber that adjoined the prioress's parlour, sat down on the carved wooden bench there and opened it.

There were the two birth certificates which she had urgently requested. Caroline Hayes, born the 23 February 1972, mother Jessica Hayes and father John Hayes, bank clerk, and Crystal Hayes, born 24th March 1973, mother Jessica Hayes, father John Hayes, bank clerk. Both girls had been born at Marsden Close, Nottinghamshire. There were then two of them, as the photograph in the Peter house had shown. She slid the certificates back in the envelope and went to see to Lilith. There was no sign that anybody had walked in the yard or entered the stable the previous night.

The van arrived just as she had finished grooming the pony.

'Good morning, Sister.' Detective Sergeant Mill brought the aura of masculinity into the stable as he put his head round the door. 'Mother Dorothy said that I'd probably find you here. We can drive the van down again to the station to take your prints and get you up to date on events and then you can bring it back here.'

'Michael Peter was here late last night,' Sister Joan told him.

'At the convent?' He looked at her sharply.

'He walked across the yard. I caught a glimpse of him through the kitchen window.'

'At what time?'

'Shortly after twelve.'

'What were you doing prowling round at that ungodly hour? I thought you were all tucked up by ten.'

'Ten-thirty, but I had leave to stay later in the chapel. I saw him for only a moment, but it was definitely him.'

'Did he see you?'

'I'm sure that he didn't. Have you arrested him?'

'We've not even questioned him yet. I want the autopsy report on Mrs Rufus before I take further steps. I have applied for a search warrant for the house and the antique shop but that will take a little while to come through. Are you ready, Sister?'

This morning he was, to her relief, brisk and businesslike, with no hint of teasing in voice or eyes. The old team, she thought, taking the keys and mounting up into the driving seat, was back in business, with an easy, undemanding friendliness between the two of them.

'So how are you then?' he said abruptly, as they were driving through the gates. 'No ill effects from our last case?'[1]

'None. We have no more money but somehow or other we manage.'

'I filled the petrol tank.'

'I wasn't hinting,' she said quickly.

'I know you weren't, but you do have a habit of helping out to great effect, so it seemed only fair to pay back a little. I must say it feels good to be back in harness. I get restless on holiday.'

'But the boys enjoyed it?'

'I think that I cramp their style,' he said wryly. 'They stayed on for a week with their mother, and I came back.'

'Their mother', not *'my wife'*. Sister Joan said, 'I got the two birth certificates from St Catherine's House. It's just as Caroline told me. You haven't—?'

'Not yet. By the time we get to the station there should be a forensic report waiting on my desk. Mother Dorothy told me that you're free for the whole day, so we can get to grips with this without you having to dash off to church. Do you often break the speed limit?'

'Sorry!' She swerved into the station yard.

There was no sign of Constable Brown when she went into the reception area. Constable Whitney greeted her with the slightly nervous politeness that non-Catholics were apt to accord nuns, and took her through to have her prints taken, while Detective Sergeant Mill disappeared into his office.

'There we are, Sister Joan!' He handed her a damp cloth and stood back. 'You've had your fingerprints taken before I understand?'

'Several times.'

'Constable Petrie was telling me, before he went down with

<hr>

[1] See *Vow of Poverty*

the measles, that you've been a big help to the Force on several occasions. It must make a bit of a change for you, being involved in a criminal investigation when you spend most of your life shut in.'

'Actually it's more the other way round,' Sister Joan said, amused. 'It's becoming a nice change for me to spend time in the enclosure.'

'Yes, Sister.' He looked slightly embarrassed at what evidently struck him as an unsuitable vein of humour in a religious, and held open the door. 'I believe that Detective Sergeant Mill would like a word.'

'The report's here.' Detective Sergeant Mill looked up from his desk. 'Rustle up some coffee, will you, Whitney? As you can see, once you've translated all the medical jargon, Mary Rufus was killed by a single blow to the back of the head, and from the angle of the wound it looks as if she was kneeling when she was hit from behind. She was found face down on the new grave.'

'She was kneeling to lay the flowers on the grave?'

'That seems a reasonable assumption. She was killed sometime in the early morning. Exact times are always hard to determine and pathologists always hate being definite. We can place it a little more exactly. She had a return ticket in her handbag to Torquay, one of those day-excursion tickets. The train left at ten-five, so she obviously called in at the cemetery on her way to the station. Michael Peter told you the truth about that anyway.'

'That's awful.' Sister Joan took the coffee that Constable Whitney handed her and gazed into its depths. 'She was carrying out a kindly gesture for a man who'd died without any family being there to pay their last respects and someone crept up behind and struck her down.'

'In the midst of her sins,' Constable Whitney said.

'D'ye think God doesn't make allowances for that?' she demanded sharply. 'Anyway she was a nice, respectable woman. She'd worked for Michael Peter for years. Has the murder weapon been found?'

'Not yet. There are plenty of large stones lying round the

cemetery. Whatever caused the injury was spherical in shape, smooth-surfaced and probably of iron or brass.'

'A large ball of some kind? Wouldn't that've been very heavy to carry?'

'The killer was a strong person,' Detective Sergeant Mill said.

'A globe? One of those balls that used to hang outside pawnbrokers' establishments?'

'Something antique?' said Constable Whitney.

'Right then!' Detective Sergeant Mill drew his pad towards him and began to doodle. 'I must say that Michael Peter appears to be involved in one way or another in all of this. First his wife stops writing to her father and sister, but sends a signal that she's in trouble to her sister. Then her father turns up dead in a chapel near the Peter house with three items that belong to him hidden in a toilet roll in Michael Peter's shower-room. Meanwhile Caroline, the sister, turns up, looking for her sister and unaware that her father's already here. Then Michael Peter's suitcase, packed with clothes that look as if they belong to his wife, is found on the embankment, and Michael Peter himself tells Sister Joan his wife is touring France with her family, which is a demonstrable lie! And then Michael Peter's housekeeper is attacked and killed in the cemetery by the grave of the man we now believe to be John Hayes, and Caroline Hayes disappears from the temporary refuge she'd found, leaving bloodstained garments in the boot of an old car. I think we'll pay him a visit. Sister?'

'I really don't want to be there,' she protested.

'You've met the man. You're more likely to pick up something pertinent in his manner or in what he says.'

'Very well.'

She was here to assist after all, but being present at the questioning of a suspect was something she had hoped to avoid.

'Is our special constable here yet?'

'Yes, sir.'

'Right, we'll leave him to hold the fort. Constable Brown has a long-standing hospital appointment today. Fluid on the knee.'

Which might well account for his ill temper, Sister Joan thought charitably as she went out to the police car with the two officers.

They drove through the town, past cemetery and station and took the ring road which curved around the jagged edges of the moor towards the rash of houses, shops and high rise apartments known still as the new estate though it had been established for years.

'The track's a bit steep. Drive up as far as you can and then park,' Detective Sergeant Mill instructed. 'This isn't going to be an official arrest, but we'll tape the interview and offer to have his solicitor present. You're there purely as an observer, Sister. If Michael Peter objects to your presence you'll have to leave.'

On a fine morning like this she ought to be riding Lilith over the sparkling grass or arranging flowers in the vase before the Holy Virgin's altar! Sister Joan lowered her eyes and wished fervently for the calm of the cloister.

'We'll park here. Whitney, bring the tape recorder. Sister, mind your step. It's a mite slippery.'

They scrambled up the last few yards of scree and reached the level ground, bearing to the right where low walls divided the rockery garden from the bracken and heather.

'Lonely place to choose to live,' Constable Whitney said.

'Michael Peter has the reputation of being a bit of a recluse,' Detective Sergeant Mill began. 'Ah, looks as if we're expected!'

'Good morning, Sister Joan!' Michael Peter had opened the gate and was already loping back into the house. 'Detective Sergeant – Mill, isn't it? And Constable—'

'Constable Whitney from Penzance.'

'A most picturesque place, but windy. Do come in. It was very good of you to come so soon. My housekeeper, Mrs Rufus, would be here to greet you but she's stayed over in Torquay.'

'Oh?' Detective Sergeant Mill's face wouldn't have looked amiss on a top poker player as they trooped into the house.

'There was a message on my answerphone when I got home last night. Rather a bother actually as the house is already getting a trifle dusty. I can make some coffee.'

'Nothing, thank you. Do you mind if we listen to the taped

message?' Detective Sergeant Mill asked.

'With pleasure, but I'm afraid I wiped it,' Michael Peter said. 'I always wipe messages once I've listened to them. She'll be back tomorrow. What I wished to call you about was a burglary.'

'You called us, sir?'

'Not ten minutes ago. You got here very fast.'

'You've been burgled?' Detective Sergeant Mill took the chair offered.

'Yes. This morning I overslept. Very unusual for me.'

'We did notice your shop hadn't been opened,' Constable Whitney said, and subsided at a glance from his superior.

'You wished to see me?' Michael Peter looked from one to the other. 'Forgive me, but I don't understand. I rang the station to report a burglary.'

'We wish to have a chat with you concerning Mrs Rufus and one or two other matters,' Detective Sergeant Mill said.

'Mrs Rufus? She's in Torquay.'

'I'm afraid she isn't, sir,' Detective Sergeant Mill said carefully. 'I'm very sorry to have to inform you that Mrs Rufus was found dead yesterday afternoon. You hadn't heard anything?'

'Nothing.'

Sister Joan, watching closely, could discern nothing in the cadaverous features but surprise and curiosity.

'You were in your shop all day?'

'Yes. No; in the afternoon I went out for a little while. There was a sale at one of the farmhouses so I drove there on the offchance of finding a bargain, but there wasn't anything that appealed to me. Mrs Rufus dead! I really feel that I ought to have been informed sooner, Detective Sergeant Mill. She had no close family, you know. No next of kin.'

'Would you mind if we switched on the tape recorder? It's simply routine these days,' Detective Sergeant Mill said.

'As I've never been questioned by the police before I'm afraid that I'm not familiar with the routine,' Michael Peter said stiffly. 'I fail to see how I can help you in any case. Mrs Rufus was getting on in years but as far as I know her health was excellent and she did the work here in her own time and at her own pace.'

'Perhaps you would like to ring your solicitor, sir, before we proceed any further?'

Detective Sergeant Mill switched on the tape recorder and looked at the older man.

'A solicitor?' Michael Peter stared at him. 'If it's a question of the bequest that was agreed between us a long time ago, and the solicitor witnessed the papers.'

'Bequest?'

'I aided Mrs Rufus and her late husband to buy their house,' Michael Peter said. 'Mr Rufus never earned a great deal and during the eighties property, even over on the new estate, was being advertised at inflated prices, so I paid for most of the house and in return, as neither had any close relatives, it was agreed that the property would revert to me after their deaths. It was all quite legal, Detective Sergeant.'

'I'm sure it was.' Detective Sergeant Mill frowned and glanced across at Sister Joan.

Michael Peter, intercepting the glance, said with a faint note of petulance in his tone, 'May I ask what Sister Joan is doing here?'

'I'm here as an observer but if you wish me to leave then of course—'

'No, no,' he said irritably. 'You might as well stay. Did you have the ill fortune to find Mrs Rufus or something? The cemetery? I thought she was going to Torquay. Was she taken ill in the cemetery or something?'

'Shall we ask the questions for the moment, sir?' Detective Sergeant Mill said. He spoke directly into the recorder, giving time and place, then looked across the pastel-shaded Aubusson carpet at the other. 'This is an informal chat, sir, but I must make it clear that the interview is being recorded and may therefore be used in evidence.'

'Evidence!' Michael Peter gave a harsh, rasping little chuckle like a nail being drawn the wrong way over silk. 'I report a burglary and the next thing I know I'm the one being questioned! I'm very sorry indeed to hear about Mrs Rufus. She was an excellent worker and a most loyal and discreet housekeeper. But I can tell you nothing about her state of health except that I don't believe she ever took a day off sick. Perhaps you'd be good enough to tell me what you propose to do about my stolen property?'

'What exactly was taken, sir?' Detective Sergeant Mill asked patiently.

'Let me begin at the beginning,' Michael Peter said pedantically, clasping one bony hand in the other and leaning forward slightly. 'Most of my valuables are kept in the shop but I do have some rather nice pieces here. I think that beautiful objects should be lived with. I have security devices in the shop and a burglar alarm here. Unfortunately I neglected to turn it on last night. I was feeling rather tired and went unthinkingly to bed.'

'That was very careless, sir, if you don't mind my saying so,' Constable Whitney interposed.

'It was exceedingly careless,' Michael Peter said severely. 'It means that the insurance company will hesitate about paying anything out. But that is my problem. I overslept this morning as I told you. It wasn't until I'd had breakfast – coffee and toast – and decided to open later on today – the shop I mean, and came in here to read the Sunday supplement – I didn't get round to it over the weekend – that I realized that I'd been robbed. There was a T'ang horse on the table. Perhaps you remember it, Sister?'

'Yes I do. It was very lovely,' Sister Joan said.

'It wasn't there,' Michael Peter continued. 'I went through into the study at the other end of the house. There are French windows there which are activated when the alarm goes off. The glass in the left-hand one was broken and the door itself unlocked. I sleep at the other side of the house and as I just told you I slept very heavily.'

'What time did you retire last night?' Detective Sergeant Mill asked.

'About eleven.'

'Check the room, Constable.' Detective Sergeant Mill nodded towards Whitney.

'Through the hall and the dining-room,' Michael Peter began. 'I haven't touched anything naturally.'

'I'll find it, sir.' Constable Whitney went out jauntily.

'So the T'ang horse is missing?' Detective Sergeant Mill said.

'And a very handsome stone ashlar,' Michael Peter said. 'From a Masonic temple, and greatly prized by me on that account. It represents regenerated man. Beautiful pink veined marble, polished to the highest lustre and an almost perfect sphere. I am more upset about losing that piece than anything!'

ELEVEN

There was silence in the room. On the wall a clock chimed sweetly. Constable Whitney came in again.

'May I have a quick word, sir?' he asked.

'Excuse us for a moment.' Detective Sergeant Mill switched off the tape recorder and rose.

'All this is very disturbing,' Michael Peter said to Sister Joan. 'I treasure my privacy, and having policemen tramping everywhere is – Mrs Rufus took great pride in the carpets.'

'They have to investigate,' Sister Joan said uncomfortably.

'And one must assist them in the course of their enquiries. However even the loss of the T'ang horse and the ashlar seems less significant when one has just heard of a sudden death. Mrs Rufus had her funny little ways but she was a very nice woman.'

The two police officers came back in. Detective Sergeant Mill sat down, switched on the tape recorder again, and said, 'Interview is resumed at—' He glanced at his watch and recorded the time.

Sister Joan, watching, wished she were elsewhere. Alan Mill had become the cool, sharp, impersonal inquisitor, his human side concealed.

'Mr Peter, I strongly advise you to have your solicitor present before we proceed,' he said.

'Are you accusing me of something?' Michael Peter's head reared up.

'Not yet, sir, but this interview is being taped in the presence of Constable Whitney and Sister Joan and may constitute evidence. I want you to understand that.'

'Oh, do get on with it, Detective Sergeant Mill!' Michael Peter said snappishly.

'Yesterday you retired to bed at about eleven o'clock. This morning, having overslept, you decided to open your antique shop this afternoon, had your breakfast and then found two items of value missing from the house and the glass of the French windows in the study smashed. The alarm hadn't triggered because you'd neglected to activate it last night. Am I right so far?'

'Yes.'

'Mr Peter, the glass that broke in the window is outside on the path.'

Sister Joan felt her hands clench into fists.

'Outside?' Mr Peter looked blank.

'Anyone breaking the glass from outside would get shards of the stuff on the carpet inside. Anyone breaking the glass from inside would force the glass outside where in fact it is. You see my point, sir?'

'I've nothing further to add,' Michael Peter said.

Detective Sergeant Mill glanced at Sister Joan and resumed, his tone becoming more casual. 'I understand that you're here alone at the moment? Your wife isn't with you?'

'She's on holiday.'

'May I ask where?'

'Touring France with her parents and her sister.'

'And their names are—?'

'Jessica and John Hayes. Her sister is called Caroline.'

'Have you ever met any of them?'

'Not yet. Crystal – that's my wife and I met and married very quickly. Letters have been exchanged but so far I haven't met them.'

'You've been married a year?'

'Ten months.'

'Isn't it a trifle unusual not to meet any of your in-laws for so long a time?'

'There's no mystery about it,' Michael Peter said irritably. 'Crystal didn't get on with her parents. This trip to France was intended to be a kind of reconciliation.'

'She left at Easter?'

'I drove her to the station myself. She was meeting her parents in London.'

'You didn't drive her all the way?'

'I use my car only for short, necessary journeys. I paid for her rail ticket by cheque. I imagine that can be checked out.'

'And you've heard nothing since?'

'I—' Michael Peter hesitated, then said flatly, 'No.'

'And you don't find that very worrying?'

'I assumed that they're travelling and haven't time to write.'

'Or telephone?'

The antique dealer was silent again.

'Let's turn to Mrs Rufus,' Detective Sergeant Mill said.

'What has Mrs Rufus to do with my wife?'

'Mrs Rufus was found dead yesterday in the cemetery. To put it in layman's terms the back of her skull had been crushed by an extremely heavy spherical object – an ashlar perhaps?'

'Good God!' Michael Peter's expression had changed. There was alarm and there was horror written across his face. 'That's dreadful! Dreadful!'

'She had gone to the cemetery with flowers which she obviously meant to put on the grave of the man found dead in the old chapel near here.'

'Sister Joan found the body. Mrs Rufus informed me. Why did Mrs Rufus put flowers on the grave?'

'Because at heart she was a very kind person,' Sister Joan said, unable to bear having to keep silence a moment longer. 'She took some flowers for the grave of a man who hadn't had any friends or relatives at his funeral. She knelt down to place the flowers on the earth and someone crept up behind her and smashed in her skull.'

'With my ashlar? That's a terrible thought.'

'And of course quite impossible,' Detective Sergeant Mill said, 'since Mrs Rufus was killed yesterday morning and your burglary didn't occur until last night. It did occur last night, didn't it, Mr Peter?'

'I think that I'd like to have my solicitor present,' Michael

Peter said. 'Switch off the tape!'

'Certainly, sir.' Detective Sergeant Mill did so. 'Do you want to continue this interview down at the station or here?'

'I've never been in a police cell in my life.' Michael Peter reared his head again, cracking his knuckles unpleasantly. 'I'll telephone for my solicitor.'

'Wouldn't it be better to have an informal chat without the tape recorder or a solicitor here?' Sister Joan ventured. 'If you can explain—'

'That's highly irregular, Sister,' Detective Sergeant Mill said.

'I know but—?' She sent him a pleading glance.

'Very well, but there'll have to be a formal interview sooner or later.'

'I'll make some coffee,' Michael Peter said.

'Go with him, Constable.' Detective Sergeant Mill waited until the door had closed behind them, then looked at Sister Joan.

'Why are we playing good cop bad cop?' she enquired.

'Is that what we're doing?' He smiled slightly. 'Well, perhaps. What's your own reading of the affair?'

'I'm in a complete muddle,' she said frankly. 'Michael Peter didn't go to bed at eleven last night – unless he got up again and came to the convent to walk round in the yard.'

'You're sure it was him?'

'Positive. I only caught a glimpse of him but he's a fairly unmistakable figure.'

'I agree with you.'

'And as you said if Mrs Rufus was killed yesterday morning it couldn't have been with the ashlar if the ashlar and the T'ang horse were only stolen last night.'

'By someone who breaks the window from the outside and manages to get all the broken glass in the garden. If there wasn't murder involved I'd say that this was an insurance scam.'

'Michael Peter has certainly been lying,' Sister Joan said, 'but I do find it hard to believe he's dishonest. He was very generous when he sold me the chalice for Father Malone.'

'How much did it cost?'

'Seven hundred and fifty pounds. It is real silver and very beautiful.'

'But not spherical in shape?'

'No, and anyway it's hidden away in the presbytery until the presentation at the children's home, so it couldn't have killed Mrs Rufus. It's irrelevant.' She broke off as Michael Peter came in, with Constable Whitney bearing the coffee tray in his wake.

'I think that I ought to be frank with you, Detective Sergeant Mill,' the former said.

'On or off the record?' Detective Sergeant Mill enquired.

'You can switch it on. And don't go through that spiel about my rights again. As I haven't done anything then I don't need a solicitor.'

'Very well.' He switched it on and looked at the older man. 'Let's start again, shall we?'

'Where?' There was an edge of weary sarcasm in the other's voice.

'You went on business to London a few days ago?'

'Yes I did.' Michael Peter looked disconcerted at the change in direction. 'I met Sister Joan on my way to the station.'

'You were carrying a large suitcase.'

'I often do carry luggage when I go away.'

'You didn't stay overnight?'

'No. As it happens I returned on the same day.'

'Without the suitcase?'

'I – yes.'

'A large suitcase corresponding to the description of the one you were carrying was found on the embankment between here and London and handed in at the station,' Detective Sergeant Mill said. 'It was found to contain a large number of garments, very expensive garments for a woman. Perhaps you'd like to start by telling us about that.'

'The suitcase was mine. The clothes belonged to my wife.'

'You will get the opportunity of seeing these items for yourself and identifying them formally. Perhaps you'd like to tell us why you discarded them?'

'Because I couldn't bear to have them in the house any longer,' Michael Peter said.

'One suitcase full? Didn't your wife have more clothes than that?' Sister Joan asked.

'She took everything else with her.'

'To France?'

'France!' He half rose, then sank back in his chair, his face twisted into a grin as he stared at her. 'France! Why don't you stop playing games with me, Sister? You know Crystal never went to France. You knew it when you came into my shop expecting to get something cheap for your wretched parish priest!'

'I don't know what you're talking about,' Sister Joan said blankly.

'Oh, don't play the innocent with me, Sister!' he said. 'You wanted a bargain and you found a way to force one out of me, didn't you? You guessed my wife wasn't in France and you made that clear to me – very clear by looking in a meaning way at my desk.'

'What desk?'

'My Napoleon desk. French. You made a comment. Something apparently innocuous but it let me know that you'd guessed and were willing to keep quiet for a price.'

'How dare you!' Her blue eyes blazing, Sister Joan sprang to her feet. 'How dare you insinuate that I'd actually stoop to a bit of discreet blackmail in order to get what I wanted? How dare you impute motives to me that I never had? I remember the desk, and I believe that I did pass some casual comment about it but I was just making light conversation! You must live in a very murky world if you think that things like blackmail are common, or that nuns will stoop to anything to get a bargain!'

'If I was wrong then naturally I apologize,' Michael Peter said stiffly.

'I should think so!' Sister Joan sat down with a decided thump.

'The interesting point,' Detective Sergeant Mill said, his face carefully unsmiling, 'is that you interpreted the remark as blackmail and you promptly paid up. You did sell Sister Joan the chalice very cheaply, didn't you?'

'So you already knew that your wife wasn't in France,' Sister Joan said.

'I don't know where Crystal is,' Michael Peter said heavily. 'She left at Easter. I did drive her to the station. She said that she was going away for a few days to think things over. Our marriage wasn't entirely happy. She was bored here. Crystal likes to go out to the theatre or dancing. I'm somewhat set in my ways.'

'Where exactly was she going?' Detective Sergeant Mill asked.

'London. She said something about going to see her father. She said that she didn't know if she was ever coming back. She had most of her things with her and I gave her sufficient money. She couldn't accuse me of being ungenerous.'

'And that was the last you heard?'

Michael Peter nodded.

'But why did you tell Mrs Rufus that she'd gone to France?' Sister Joan asked.

'It was the first thing came into my head. If I'd said she had gone to visit her father, even Mrs Rufus would've begun to wonder if she stayed away too long. Were she touring in France that gave me time to decide what to do – what to say.'

'You didn't want Mrs Rufus to know that she'd left you?'

'I have my pride,' he said.

'But surely you worried about her?'

'I went to London a month ago. I had business there anyway so I went to the flat where she'd lived with her father. He's something of an invalid. Was. If is. The man in the chapel—?'

'He was almost certainly John Hayes,' Detective Sergeant Mill said.

'I was afraid of that. I wrote to him and asked him to come down and meet me. He was receiving treatment on a fairly regular basis at the Florence Nightingale Heart Unit, and I sent the letter there.'

'Why not to his home address?'

'I thought his wife might get hold of it,' Michael Peter said.

'Jessica Hayes died some years back,' Detective Sergeant Mill said.

'That's not possible. Crystal was very fond of her mother. She often spoke of her. I didn't want to upset Mrs Hayes by

letting her know that Crystal and I were having any problems,
so I sent the letter to the hospital and asked them to hold it for
him. Then I went to London to his home address—'
   'Had you received a reply to your letter in the meantime?'
   'Nothing, but he had received it. I rang the Heart Unit just to
be sure. Then I grew tired of waiting so I went up to London. It
was a complete waste of time. They'd moved house and
apparently left no forwarding address. I guessed then that
Crystal wouldn't come back to me. You say her mother is dead?
I cannot understand why she would do that.'
   'Your wife seems to have been a rather unusual kind of
person,' Sister Joan said.
   'You never met her,' Michael Peter said, 'so you can't
presume to judge. She's a lovely young woman, a lovely
person. We hit it off at once when we first met. It was at a trade
fair and she was the most beautiful thing there. I couldn't take
my eye off her.'
   For an instant he looked younger, more vulnerable. Sister
Joan said, 'You were in love with her?'
   'I adored her,' he said simply. 'You know I've never had
much success with the ladies. Had I been a Catholic I daresay
I'd have ended my days in the religious life, the last refuge of
the unloved.'
   'Oh, is that what you think?' Sister Joan began.
   'Thank you, Sister.' Detective Sergeant Mill sent her an
amused glance. 'So you had no luck with ladies, Mr Peter?'
   'Not that I tried very hard. Mother was the most marvellous
company right up until her death, and she loved this place so
much. "I'm your queen of the castle, aren't I, Michael?" she
used to say. She was too. I couldn't have brought another
woman into the house while she lived here. It would've hurt
her feelings terribly. Mrs Rufus, being married and not sleeping
in, was different, of course. She and Mother got on very well.
Now, where was I?'
   'Not having any luck with the ladies,' Sister Joan said
sweetly.
   'None at all,' he said. 'Not that I tried very hard, but it was
five years since Mother had died and it does get very quiet in

the evenings. And then I met Crystal and it was as if we'd known each other for years. I adored her.'

'But she was bored here, sir?' Constable Whitney asked.

'I offered to take her to the shop with me. She'd have made a splendid saleslady, but she never wanted to go into town. I took her to the shop, of course, and she loved all the things there, but she considered it unwise for husband and wife to spend twenty-four hours a day together, and she was probably right. She stayed in the house instead.'

'And then she left?' Detective Sergeant Mill leaned his chin on his hand and regarded the other steadily.

'I pretended that she'd gone to France. I almost believed it myself. Then when I found the Hayes family had moved I knew she wouldn't come back. It was a terrible shock even though I'd begun to feel that she never would come back. I wouldn't have given her a divorce, you know. Oh no, Mother reared me to have somewhat traditional values. She prided herself on the fact that no divorced woman had ever crossed her threshold.'

'So you put the rest of her clothes in a suitcase and threw it out of the train?'

'No, of course not!' Michael Peter looked indignant. 'Flinging things from moving vehicles is a most dangerous practice. It can cause very nasty accidents.'

'I wish you'd tell that to some of the younger generation who live on the estate,' Detective Sergeant Mill said. 'So what did you do?'

'Alighted a couple of stations up the line, waited until the platform was deserted, and then climbed a little way down the embankment and left it there. Then I caught the next train back. I had to wait a very long time for it, so I had a light meal on the station. Not a very appetising meal.'

'What made you say that the dead man found in the chapel was John Hayes?' Detective Sergeant Mill enquired.

'I rang up the hospital a couple of weeks ago. I learned that he was due in for further treatment and I asked him to telephone me – that is to say I gave my home number to the receptionist at the Heart Unit. He never rang and he never came. When I rang again a couple of days ago – Saturday it was – they told me that he'd called briefly at the unit, taken down my number, and gone away saying that he'd be back later, but hadn't returned at all. After that I began to put two and two together. A man with no identification dying of a heart attack so near to my house seemed like an odd coincidence.'

'You didn't mention your suspicions to the police, sir,' Constable Whitney reproached.

'Then I would've had to go into detail concerning my private life, my marital problems. I'm a very private man and—'

'So you've told us,' Detective Sergeant Mill said. 'You ought to have come forward, sir. I take it that John Hayes didn't ring you or come to the house?'

'No, he didn't.'

'Then you'd be very surprised to learn that his credit card, and his watch and his pen with his name on it were found here in your house?'

'Here? Where?'

'Hidden in the centre of a toilet roll in your shower-room,' Sister Joan said. 'I came across them accidentally when I used your toilet on Sunday.'

'You didn't say anything!' His eyes accused her.

'Sister Joan is assisting with our enquiries,' Detective Sergeant Mill said smoothly. 'The discovery placed her in a very awkward position. Naturally she handed them over to us. She also informed his daughter.'

'I had to tell her that her father was probably dead,' Sister Joan said.

'Daughter. You've seen Crystal? You've met my wife?'

Michael Peter begun to rise excitedly, then sat down again, clenching his jaw.

'Her sister is desperately worried about her,' Sister Joan said. 'Neither Caroline nor her father have heard anything from her since Easter.'

'You've been to London? You know where they live?'

'Caroline came to me for advice,' Sister Joan said. 'She wanted to find out where her sister was. She had no idea that her father had broken his appointment at the Heart Unit and travelled here. Her main concern has been to stay out of sight. She seemed to fear that some harm had befallen Crystal at your hands. I'm sorry but that was definitely the impression I received from her.'

'Caroline here?' Michael Peter flexed his fingers, cracking each joint in a series of small pistol shots. 'Caroline Hayes here?'

'Why did you pretend there'd been a burglary, sir?' Constable Whitney asked.

'There was!' Michael Peter's sharp cheekbones flushed a dull red. 'The night before last—'

'That would be Sunday night, would it?'

'Yes, Sunday night. I was tired and worried about Crystal and a little peeved because Mrs Rufus had mentioned she might go to Torquay, which meant the house would get a trifle dusty, and I neglected to turn on the alarm when I went to bed. Yesterday morning I discovered the T'ang horse and the ashlar were both missing.'

'Then why not report the theft immediately?'

'Because I felt a complete fool,' Michael Peter said. 'Just think of it! I am an antique dealer. Every day I deal with very valuable artefacts. I am responsible for their security. If they are stolen I lose profits. I don't like to lose profits.'

'So you waited another twenty-four hours before you reported it?'

'I was in a quandary,' Michael Peter said. 'I had to open the shop and Mrs Rufus wasn't coming in and so I waited. I thought that some idea might occur to me, and then last night I got it! If I smashed the glass and made it look like a break-in—'

'Mr Peter, why don't you stop playing games with us?' Detective Sergeant Mill said. 'First you pretend the items were stolen last night. Then you tell us it happened two nights ago and you didn't want to admit to the police that you'd neglected to set the alarm, so you faked the break-in this morning, but the moment we arrive you inform us that you forgot to set the alarm anyway. What really happened?'

'I forgot to turn on the alarm on Sunday night and yesterday morning I discovered the T'ang horse and the ashlar were gone. I waited, decided to stage a break-in.'

'Very clumsily,' Detective Sergeant Mill said. 'Sister Joan would have managed it better.'

'I'm not used to telling lies,' Michael Peter said. 'Mother detested liars. Give her a murderer or a thief rather than a liar she used to say.'

'And are you a murderer?' Detective Sergeant Mill enquired softly.

'Of course not! I couldn't kill anything,' he said. 'Mrs Rufus used to have a little joke with me because I cannot stand even to gut fish. You can't seriously believe that I could smash somebody's head in? For what reason? Mrs Rufus was an excellent housekeeper. I really don't know how I am going to be able to manage without her!'

'Mr Peter, can you give us any further information concerning your wife's whereabouts?' Detective Sergeant Mill asked.

'No! No, no, and again no! Now that you know she's missing why aren't you out looking for her? Why are you asking me these fruitless questions?'

'Mr Peter, did you try to fake a break-in because you were afraid that Crystal had sneaked in and taken the horse and the ashlar?' Sister Joan asked.

'She wouldn't have meant to steal,' he said quickly. 'Crystal always loved the T'ang horse and the ashlar. She used to sit and stroke the polished marble of the ashlar over and over, and smile a little as if she were caressing a – someone else.'

'So you think she may have come back and taken them?'

'I wouldn't want to get her into trouble,' Michael Peter said miserably. 'I'd be glad for her to have them, but if someone else did take them – I was in a quandary, you see. I simply didn't know what was best to say.'

'The truth is always helpful, sir,' Constable Whitney observed.

'It was very foolish of me. Naturally if my wife did take them then I won't bring any charges against her.'

'If we find the ashlar was used to batter Mrs Rufus then the matter will be out of your hands, sir,' Detective Sergeant Mill said.

'You're not suggesting that Crystal—' Michael Peter stared at him, his mouth working.

'I'm suggesting nothing, Mr Peter,' Detective Sergeant Mill said. 'Until we find Mrs Peter we can't say anything definite. Her sister is very worried for her safety.'

'You said she was here? Her sister was here?'

'Was here,' Detective Sergeant Mill said.

'She's run off again?' Michael Peter gave a sarcastic little laugh. 'Well, from all I've heard about her that's typical! What my mother would've called a flibbertigibbet, Detective Sergeant Mill. Blonde you know.'

'Caroline is blonde?' Sister Joan said.

'I have a photograph of the two of them together, taken a couple of years ago. I'll get it. One moment!'

He had left the room and returned with the framed portrait before Sister Joan had had time to say a word.

'I've seen this picture before,' she said now. 'I assumed that Crystal was the fair-haired one.'

'Did Mr Peter indicate which was his wife?' Detective Sergeant Mill asked.

'No, he didn't, but I thought—'

'My wife is brown-haired,' Michael Peter said.

'But—' Sister Joan caught the detective sergeant's eye and was silent.

'Mother would certainly never have tolerated a blonde around the house!' Michael Peter said. 'Crystal has brown hair, drawn back into a rather elegant pleat. She was one of the hostesses at a trade fair when we met. Run by one of the more elite galleries. Crystal is a lady, I assure you!'

TWELVE

'I never felt so stupid in my entire life!' Sister Joan said.

They sat in Detective Sergeant Mill's office, coffee cups and the remains of a large plate of cheese sandwiches between them.

'You weren't to know.' Detective Sergeant Mill sounded consoling.

'I ought to have checked up which one in the photograph was Crystal,' Sister Joan said. 'When someone tells me that her name's Caroline I don't expect her to turn out to be her sister!'

They had all driven down to the station where Michael Peter had made a formal statement and been released pending further enquiries and had gone off to open up his shop.

'Let's look at the statement from the beginning.' Detective Sergeant Mill picked up the typescript and read it slowly.

' "My name is Michael Peter and I'm forty-five years old. I live at Pebble Heights on East Moor, and also own the antique shop called by my name in Tor Alley. I have lived in this area for over twenty years. Last year at a trade fair I met Crystal Hayes who was working as hostess at the event. We were married at Chelsea Register Office a month later and came immediately to Cornwall. Crystal told me that she and her family did not enjoy close links though she was fond of her older sister, Caroline. The marriage was happy at first but deteriorated later. Crystal was bored in the country and had no desire to share in the antique business. I blame myself for not being more attentive to her. My housekeeper, Mrs Rufus, came up to the house every day but my wife had little in common with her. There was, I understand, a slight altercation between them once concerning my wife's habit of playing popular music rather loudly. I can understand that such music would appeal to a young woman, and Mrs Rufus made no further complaints." '

'Mrs Rufus mentioned that she played pop music all day,' Sister Joan recalled.

He resumed his reading. ' "At Easter Crystal told me that she wanted to go and visit her parents and her sister and I drove her to the station and bought her ticket to London. I noticed that she took most of her clothes with her and the suspicion entered my mind that she might decide not to return. I said nothing to her but I did tell Mrs Rufus that Crystal was touring France with her family. That would save face if Crystal did stay away for a long time. After a month during which I received only one brief, hurried call I went to London myself to the apartment where the Hayes, according to my wife, lived. I was informed they had moved away leaving no forwarding address. I returned home and endeavoured to contact John Hayes, Crystal's father, through the Florence Nightingale Heart Unit, I was informed by them that my message to him suggesting a meeting had been passed on but I heard nothing. When I did learn that Sister Joan of the Order of the Daughters of Compassion had found the body of an unidentified man in the abandoned chapel near my house I did wonder if it might have been John Hayes. May I say at this point that I had no idea that certain articles belonging to John Hayes were hidden in my shower-room." ' Detective Sergeant Mill looked up. 'Do you believe that?'

'It's feasible,' Sister Joan said. 'The toilet roll was in a basket filled with clean toilet rolls. I'd never have found it if I hadn't knocked the basket over. I imagine Mrs Rufus saw to the replenishment of household goods etcetera. I don't think Michael Peter is a domestic animal.'

'Right, let's see.' He returned to the statement. ' "On Sunday evening I went to bed and forgot to activate the alarm in the house. I was still worried about Crystal and anxious too because I had previously packed her remaining garments into an old suitcase and left them on the embankment. It was a foolish gesture, prompted by depression at her continued absence and by annoyance since, whatever my shortcomings as a partner, I had always been a generous husband. On Monday morning I discovered that a T'ang horse and a marble ashlar had been taken from the house during the night. Crystal had always admired these two ornaments and I suspected that she might have returned in order to take them. I said nothing to anybody but last night I began to fear that there had been a burglary by people unknown to me. It occurred to me that I might stage a break-in and telephone the police, giving the impression it had only just happened. It was a foolish move which I now regret." '

'Because he's been made to look a fool, I suppose,' Sister Joan said.

' "Regarding my housekeeper, Mrs Rufus. She has worked for me for nearly twenty years and has been satisfactory in every way. She intimated recently that she intended to go to Torquay for the day and was due to go on Monday. On Monday evening I came home to find a brief message on my telephone answering machine from Mrs Rufus to inform me she was staying in Torquay for a second day. I now know that Mrs Rufus could not have left that message since she had been killed on Monday morning before setting out for the station. I do recall thinking that her voice sounded slightly indistinct but that is with hindsight and as I wiped the tape according to my usual practice then I have no proof." '

'It's still feasible,' Sister Joan said thoughtfully.

'I'm leaving out the various dates,' Detective Sergeant Mill said. 'He seems pretty vague about them anyway. Shall I go on?'

'Please.'

' "I have been asked to supply a description of my wife Crystal. She is slim, of average height, with a pale complexion, brown eyes and light brown hair which she usually ties back. She is quiet and ladylike in manner. I am given to understand that she is in the area. I suspected that she might be when the T'ang horse and the ashlar were taken from my house. Indeed on Monday evening I walked up to the convent. I am not a Catholic and have little sympathy with papistry, but I had met Sister Joan who seemed to know, from remarks she made during a sale transaction between us, something about my wife, and I had it in mind to request an interview, but when I reached the convent everybody seemed to have retired, and after walking about for some time I walked home again without ringing the bell." '

'If someone had rung the bell at that particular moment I'd have had a fit,' Sister Joan said.

'No you wouldn't, Sister. You're the last woman in the world to panic,' Detective Sergeant Mill retorted. 'What were you doing up so late anyway? You said something about chapel.'

'Extra praying time. That's my main task you know. Helping the police is—'

'An interesting hobby?' He cocked an eyebrow.

'Get on with Michael Peter's statement.' She grinned back at him.

' "I would finally like to state that I have no knowledge about the death of Mrs Rufus and no knowledge of my wife's present whereabouts. I shall be very relieved to hear from her so that we can meet and discuss the differences that have arisen between us. My own feelings for her are undiminished." '

'He said he adored her,' Sister Joan said as Detective Sergeant Mill laid down the typescript. 'Adoration bestowed on the wrong person can be dangerous.'

'I can't visualize Michael Peter carrying out a *crime passionel*,' he objected.

'Still waters run deep,' Sister Joan said sententiously.

'We haven't arrested him.' Detective Sergeant Mill rested his chin on his linked hands and frowned slightly. 'Constable Whitney and our special constable were a mite disappointed. The search warrants are through so I'll go along to the house and the shop and see what's to be found. Will you come?'

'I think you can search a couple of places without my help,' Sister Joan said.

'In that case let's take a swift look at the sequence of events that involve Crystal Peter. She leaves her middle-aged husband, possibly for good, and then comes back here giving her sister's name and looking for herself. She even goes to the local police station to make enquiries and when they don't take her seriously she recalls a newspaper article in which your name appears and comes to the convent.'

'Funking it a couple of times,' Sister Joan reminded him.

'Well, her story must've sounded slightly peculiar.' He cast her a glance. 'I take it that if I'd been around you'd have enlisted my help?'

'Yes, of course. I would've told Constable Petrie if he hadn't gone down with the measles.'

'If your convent ever gets burgled,' he said dryly, 'and Petrie and I aren't around I do hope you'll trust whoever is manning the station with a prompt report.'

'Yes, of course I would!' Sister Joan said. 'This wasn't a simple matter. She was really scared of Michael Peter's discovering she was in the neighbourhood. She gave me the distinct impression that she believed some harm had come to her sister at his hands and since I'd already been told that Crystal was touring France with her family and that clearly wasn't true then I was inclined to believe her.'

'Her real worry must've been that Michael Peter might see her and recognize her.'

'But she did go to the police. If they'd taken her seriously – and now she seems to have disappeared.'

'There's no seems about it,' he said. 'She vanished and left a bloodstained sweater and skirt behind.'

'In the boot of a car and the boot was wedged open so that anyone could've found the clothes.'

'We've had the further forensic report on the clothes,' he said. 'It arrived early today. I intended to tell you about it but we got sidetracked by the involvement in the Peter house with the supposed burglary and all the rest of it. I might not have arrested Michael Peter for murder yet but I'm tempted to book him for wasting police time!'

'What does the report say?'

'The blood on the clothes belongs to two groups. Group A which is incidentally the blood group to which Mrs Rufus belonged and Group O, which is more common. Of course, they'll find out a great deal more once they get the DNA readings. I've requested a full analysis.'

'Could Mrs Rufus have grappled with her attacker?'

'She was struck from behind. The first blow would've killed her. Her blood would've spurted up and sprayed the murder weapon and possibly the murderer too if they were stooping low at the time.'

'A short person?'

'Short or tall they'd still have stooped. If the ashlar was used that's too heavy to hold at arm's length for more than a second or two.'

'Then it was probably someone else's blood on the skirt and sweater as well as that of Mrs Rufus?'

'It means doing a lot of checking,' he said with a trace of irritation. 'I'm hoping that Crystal or Caroline was a blood donor or had an operation so that we find some record.'

'What we need are identity cards with our DNA number stamped on them!'

'Don't mock.' He smiled at her. 'Big Brother is active enough already. Where are you off?'

'I've a convent to go to. Mother Dorothy gave me permission to stay if I was needed, but if I stay much longer the Police Federation will start charging me rent.'

'I'll be in touch then.'

'Don't get up. I know my way out.'

She left him rereading the statement again and went out to where the van was parked. There were echoes of things not spoken nagging the edges of her mind. Constable Brown. Why should his broad, self-satisfied face jump into her thoughts? Constable Petrie. The young woman in the shabby brown clothes. Was she dead or alive? She had to be somewhere. She had to be Crystal. Then what had happened to Caroline?

Crystal murdered her sister and is trying to frame her husband for the killing? Why had Mrs Rufus been killed then? That had to have been premeditated if the murder weapon had been the ashlar. Nobody takes a stroll with a heavy marble sphere in their arms. But Mrs Rufus had apparently bought some flowers and gone to the cemetery on impulse on her way to catch the train to Torquay.

She drove past the schoolhouse where a police van was parked. No doubt they were still taking photographs and hunting for clues. So far all the clues pointed to Michael Peter.

He'd lied about his wife's trip to France. He'd discarded a suitcase full of her clothes on the embankment. He'd tried to arrange a meeting with John Hayes and swore he'd never actually talked to him though John Hayes's possessions had been hidden in his shower-room and a corpse who was almost certainly John Hayes himself had been lying nearby in the old chapel. He'd lied about the burglary, ostensibly to protect his wife's reputation but if he'd used that ashlar himself then he needed to provide himself with an alibi.

'Did you get any luncheon, Sister Joan?' Sister Teresa asked as she entered the kitchen.

'A cheese sandwich and coffee,' Sister Joan said, bending to pat Alice who bounded up with tail wagging furiously. 'Do you need any help here now that I'm back?'

'Sister Marie and I are managing beautifully. Oh, if you do have time you could take the new jar of coffee and the sugar over to the postulancy. I haven't had time yet.'

'I'll take it now.'

'You'd better take the wheelie bag then,' Sister Teresa said. 'There's a pile of mugs that seem to have walked over here and really live over there. Thank you, Sister.'

With Alice frolicking at her heels and making mock assaults on the wheelie bag to prove she could be fierce if she put her mind to it Sister Joan walked along the side of the enclosure garden and through the shrubbery walk to the sunken tennis court. It was weed-grown now, a tattered net hanging forlornly by a rusting post, the sound of youthful laughter and the smack of ball on racquet long silent. At the far side the plain little house which had once been a dower cottage and was used as a postulancy by the Order wore a gay aspect with the first white flowers of the creeper that clung to its façade bursting into bloom. There was only one postulant here now. Bernadette would be starting the first year of her novitiate in the autumn.

She would exchange her pink smock and white bonnet for a grey habit with a black veil, grow her hair two inches and be permitted to speak to her fellow nuns, but she would continue to sleep in the postulancy. It was a great pity that the Order couldn't attract more candidates.

'Sister Joan, how lovely to see you!'

From anyone else the greeting might have been interpreted as a snide comment on the periods of time she'd recently spent out of the enclosure, but Sister Hilaria was incapable of spite. Her long face was wreathed in a smile and her large hands, hands so much at variance with her dreaming eyes, seized the handle of the wheelie bag.

'I'll see to that, Sister dear! What a blessing these things are when the legs begin to go – not that you need worry about that yet! Sister Teresa never forgets to replenish the coffee and sugar. Such a dear girl!'

'She's a very fine lay sister,' Sister Joan agreed, relinquishing the wheelie bag. 'Sister Marie too.'

'And Sister Bernadette will make a splendid novice.' Sister Hilaria beamed as she lugged the bag over the step into the narrow passage. 'I am very pleased with her progress, very pleased indeed. Come into the kitchen, Sister. It's time for a cup of coffee. You'll have one?'

She was already filling the kettle.

'Thank you, Sister.'

She was already awash with coffee but Sister Hilaria's life within the community was a lonely one, spent mainly in the postulancy with whichever novices were under her training at the time. On the rare occasions she expressed a wish for company it was kinder to indulge her.

'Bernadette is at her devotions,' Sister Hilaria said, pulling up a stool to the table that stood against one wall of the little kitchen where novice mistress and postulant made their simple breakfasts and odd cups of tea and coffee. 'She shall have her cup afterwards. Well, Sister, are you close to solving your case?'

Sister Joan opened her mouth, then closed it again. Sister Hilaria might live most of her life on the spiritual level but on occasion could prove that she was as aware of what was going on in the world about her as any of them.

'You are helping the police again, aren't you?' Sister Hilaria pushed the biscuit tin towards her.

'No, thank you, Sister. Yes in a way. I'm helping the police though, so far, not very effectively.'

'It must earn you great merit in Heaven when you sacrifice your time with God so cheerfully in order to bring criminals to justice,' Sister Hilaria said. 'I give thanks daily that no such outside interruptions are inflicted on me, but then if they were I would be quite inadequate to deal with them. I was always more Mary than Martha.'

'Wasn't it Mary who chose the better part?'

'So Our Blessed Lord said, Sister, but I cannot help feeling a little reinterpretation wouldn't go amiss,' Sister Hilaria said. 'After all there was Martha rushing round trying to provide a meal for a crowd of very hungry disciples, all wanting to wash their hands and get the desert sand out of their hair, and there was Mary, seated in the best place and listening. I do sometimes wonder if our reading of the event hasn't been mistaken. I don't believe Our Dear Lord was rebuking Martha and praising her sister. I believe that He was complimenting Martha on her hard work and teasing Mary a little because she'd chosen what in modern parlance might be called a cushy number. So your helping outside the convent can only enhance your spiritual standing.'

'How did you hear about the present case?' Sister Joan asked.

'How did I hear?' Sister Hilaria stared at her for a moment. 'I can't imagine, Sister dear. Someone said something. Something about a new postulant? Yes, that was it. Padraic Lee came over with fish while Bernadette and I were gathering flowers. Sometime recently, if I'm not mistaken. I saw one of our Sisters as we were—'

'It was me,' Sister Joan said.

'Of course it must've been,' Sister Hilaria said, nodding. 'She resembled you so closely. Anyway Padraic stopped to greet us as he always does. Such a nice fellow! He asked me if we were expecting a – new recruit was the way he put it. Rather a happy phrase. Soldiers of the Lord, carrying banners! Bernadette and I had a most interesting little chat about it later on.'

'Why would Padraic Lee think we were expecting a new novice?' Sister Joan asked.

'Oh, a young woman, looking rather plain and shabby – isn't it strange how so many people imagine that only plain, shabby females enter the religious life? Well, anyway he'd given this young woman a lift in his van and left her at the convent gates before going round to the back to deliver his catch to Sister Perpetua. Poached, I suspect, but delicious all the same. He assumed the young woman had gone up to the front door. I told him that no new postulants were expected. Mother Dorothy would certainly have informed me about it. She knows what great pleasure it would give me. I pray so hard for new candidates to the Order so that Our Blessed Lord may be more widely adored, but I daresay He's busy with the crisis in Bosnia at present. Anyway it did occur to me that as there was no newcomer and it wasn't a general visiting day and you were not here at lunchtime, so clearly you were involved on a case.'

'A very puzzling one,' Sister Joan said.

'Oh, you'll sort it out, Sister dear!' Sister Hilaria patted her arm. 'Has it to do with the body that was found? Or was that last year?'

'There was a body found in an old chapel on East Moor and then a woman from the estate was found murdered in the cemetery. And another person has disappeared.'

'A person you know?'

'The young woman to whom Padraic Lee gave a lift.'

'Oh dear, I am sorry to hear it.' Sister Hilaria clucked her tongue. 'Padraic did mention that she seemed very nervous. You know there's a theory that the harder you run away from what you fear the sooner it will overtake you! More coffee, Sister?'

'No, thank you, Sister. I have to get back to the main house.'

'Don't go back empty handed.' Sister Hilaria reached down to the cupboard beneath the little sink. 'Sister Teresa was only saying the other day that she needed some plant pots in which to try her hand at growing some indoor herbs, and Sister

Martha is short of them herself – there are four big ones here. Can you take them back?'

'Yes, of course, Sister.'

'These wheeled bags are a godsend, aren't they? One can carry quite heavy objects around without undue fatigue,' Sister Hilaria said. 'Thank you again, Sister Joan.'

'Thank you,' Sister Joan answered slowly as she tugged the wheelie bag over the step again. Behind her she could hear Sister Hilaria's voice raised.

'Sister Bernadette, come and have your cup of coffee now, there's a good child. Adoring God is one thing but nagging Him to take notice is quite another!'

'There's a telephone call for you,' Sister Marie announced, as Sister Joan went into the kitchen. 'Detective Sergeant Mill's on the line.'

'Thank you, Sister.' Sister Joan hurried into the corridor and took the receiver.

'Sister Joan speaking,' she said crisply.

'We've just received a further bit of information from Michael Peter,' Detective Sergeant Mills' voice informed her. 'He told us that Crystal, his wife, had given blood sometime last year. Her blood group is type O. I know that isn't conclusive but it certainly seems to indicate that whoever killed Mrs Rufus also killed Crystal. We're keeping a very close eye on Michael Peter.'

'Have you searched the house and the shop yet?' she asked.

'We did a preliminary search but we'll be back in the morning,' he said. 'That shop has some wonderful things in it. I can't say I was very keen on the exhibition at the back though. A trifle ghoulish in my opinion.'

'But you haven't found anything significant?'

'Not yet, but this was only a preliminary search. My own feeling is that if he has done away with his wife he won't have left any evidence in the shop. He regards that place as a shrine to beauty – very expensive beauty. He'd not dream of cluttering it up with a corpse.'

'The house?'

'Full of mementoes of Mother dearest.' His voice was wry.

'She seems to have been one of those helpless little women who keep a tight rein on their beloved sons. Of course he adored her and then transferred that adoration to his young wife. What happens if the wife proves unworthy and the adoration sours?'

'I don't suppose you found a wheelie bag in the house or the shop?' Sister Joan asked.

'No, we didn't. Why?'

'They're handy for carrying heavy objects about,' Sister Joan said. 'God bless.'

THIRTEEN

Someone was breaking the Grand Silence. Sister Joan woke to a low, insistent tapping on her door and sat up, blinking into the darkness as she said, 'Yes?'

'Sister Mary Concepta is taken bad.' Sister Perpetua opened the door a crack. 'Mother Dorothy is up and has summoned an ambulance. Can you come?'

'Give me five minutes.'

The door closed as she got out of bed and pulled up the blind sufficiently to admit the greyish light of early dawn while she dressed herself. The little steel fob watch on her habit informed her it was 3.30, another hour and a half before Sister Teresa mounted the staircase with her wooden rattle to give the first saluation of the day.

Both she and Sister Marie were apparently still sound asleep in their lay cells that opened off the kitchen. A light was on in the infirmary and Mother Dorothy was seated by Sister Mary Concepta whose face was contorted with silent pain. From the adjoining bed Sister Gabrielle, nightcap slightly askew, a shawl round her shoulders, kept up a fiercely whispered monologue.

'Don't you dare up and die on us, Mary Concepta! There's not much the matter with you beyond a touch of indigestion. I warned you about taking that pickled onion with your cheese. Didn't I warn you about taking that pickled onion? You always were one to make a fuss about nothing!'

'I've put an aspirin under her tongue,' Sister Perpetua said. 'That often helps at the onset of an attack. That sounds like the ambulance now! I'll direct them to the back. No sense in waking everybody up!'

She hurried out into the yard. Mother Dorothy, glancing at Sister Joan, said, 'I believe it's no more than a touch of angina. Very alarming when it occurs in the middle of the night. Sister Perpetua will stay with Sister Gabrielle.'

'Why? I'm neither sick nor helpless!' Sister Gabrielle broke in.

'Sister Perpetua will only start trying to issue instructions to the medical staff and that annoys them,' Mother Dorothy said. 'Play along with me on this, Sister.'

'Well, if you put it that way!' Sister Gabrielle lapsed into silence.

Ambulance attendants were starting to look younger, Sister Joan thought, as two of them came in, fresh faced as the morning that hadn't quite dawned. They were lifting Sister Mary Concepta on to a stretcher. Sister Joan gave Sister Gabrielle a reassuring nod.

'Don't you worry, Sister, we'll have her back here in no time at all,' she said.

'Complaining about her imaginary aches and pains I daresay,' Sister Gabrielle said, scowling.

In the yard Sister Perpetua said, 'But as the infirmarian it's my duty to be with Sister Mary Concepta.'

'Sister Mary Concepta is in excellent hands and Sister Joan will keep us informed of her progress,' Mother Dorothy said, coming out of the kitchen. 'I am more concerned about Sister Gabrielle at the moment. She has had a shock and needs very careful watching so you're really needed here.'

'I'll make us all a nice cup of tea,' Sister Perpetua said. 'Oh, these are Sister Mary Concepta's heart tablets, Sister Joan. You'd better show them to the doctor.'

'Don't worry, Sister.'

Sister Joan climbed up into the ambulance, then climbed down again.

'Wouldn't it be better if I followed in the van?' she said. 'Sister Mary Concepta will almost certainly be kept in hospital for several days and I've no way of getting back.'

'In my youth,' Sister Perpetua observed, on her way back into the kitchen, 'we thought nothing of a five-mile walk!'

'Take the van. God bless, Sister.' Mother Dorothy scooped up Alice who had come out to see what the unaccustomed activity was all about and went indoors again.

Sister Joan nodded at the ambulance attendant who went round to the driving seat and herself hurried to start up the van.

The moors had a strange, dreamlike aspect as the light grew and spread, patches of dark shadow becoming clumps of gorse and bramble, crouching shapes resolving themselves into bushes. The grass had lost its colour and was a pale, translucent grey.

The town wasn't yet astir. Driving along the High Street on the way to the hospital she could see the ancient town more clearly, the stone cottages and occasional black and white timbered building coming into their own again before the morning traffic began. Ahead of her the ambulance swerved into the avenue leading up to the local hospital.

In hospitals one waited. Sister Joan found an inconspicuous seat in the large reception area and sat down, folding her hands, lowering her eyes, preparing to unite herself mentally with the source of healing. Around her nurses and orderlies padded on noiseless soles and young men in short white coats breezed through.

'Sister Joan?'

A middle-aged man stood before her, grey hair sleeked back from a thin, clever face.

'Doctor?' She rose at once, bracing herself.

'Mr Evans. I'm a specialist in heart diseases.'

'Is Sister Mary Concepta going to be all right?' she asked tensely.

'She has severe angina, and she's not exactly a spring chicken, Sister.' He smiled slightly. 'However she's in no immediate danger. I have advised them to keep her here for a few days, but I'm fairly confident that she'll recover from this latest attack. Have you had any breakfast?'

'We have breakfast at eight.'

'You'll have coffee now. The cafeteria is open all night. Come along.'

He had the habit of command, she thought, following him obediently along a broad corridor and through several sets of glass doors to an area that was all rubber flooring and plastic-topped tables.

'Sit down. I'll get it.' He went to the counter where two women in green overalls were serving drinks.

'Thank you, Mr Evans.' She sipped the cappuccino with an unaccustomed feeling of sinful luxury.

'You look as if you need it.' Seating himself opposite her, he ladled sugar into his own cup and said, 'You nuns must be tough. I've treated several in my time and they all seem to recover speedily from whatever ails them.'

'Are you a local man?'

'No, I'm only here until the end of this week. I've developed a new technique for stimulating the heart without sending all the other organs into overdrive, and I've been giving a few lectures to the medical staff here. Whether the hospital managers will release the funds necessary to carry out the treatment remains to be seen. I've also done some practical work with the patients themselves which has been a nice change for me. Normally I'm based at the Florence Nightingale Heart Unit in—'

'Did you know John Hayes?' she broke in impulsively.

'Hayes.' He frowned slightly and she could almost see the files of his memory ticking over. 'Widower with two daughters. I treated him about three – four years ago. After that I had a couple of years in the States, research project, before returning to the unit. He was the last patient I treated before I flew out there which is probably why I remember him. I've not seen him recently. He was due for a check up if my memory serves me aright.'

'He died.'

'That's a shame.' He had the look of a man who had been personally cheated. 'Yes, he had an enlarged heart. Of course a transplant might've been possible but his general state of health wasn't good. It would've been extremely risky. Yes, he was a nice fellow. Very quiet and gentlemanly. His two daughters were his main interest in life. He was anxious for them both to get on.

'The younger one. She had an unusual name. Crystal? Yes, Crystal. I had quite an argument with her as a matter of fact. She was one of those rather tiresome young women who consider that animal rights take precedence over human ones. Rushed off on various demonstrations I believe. I say it was an argument but I cut her short pretty sharply – excuse me, Sister.'

He rose and went across to another white-coated man who had just entered and was looking about him. There was a brief consultation before Mr Evans returned to the table.

'It appears that I'm needed,' he said. 'No, not for your fellow nun. Finish your coffee and then tell Sister that you have my leave to look in on her. Nice meeting you. No, don't get up.'

He shook hands briefly and went out with the other doctor. Sister Joan drank the rest of her cappuccino and indulged herself by licking the last of the froth on the spoon.

Going out into the corridor again she looked round for some sign that would direct her to Intensive Care. She'd visited the hospital before and managed to find her way around but this was a different wing of the complex of buildings.

'May I help you, Sister?' A young nurse had paused to speak to her.

'I'm trying to find my way to the Intensive Care Unit,' Sister Joan said. 'I was told that Sister Mary Concepta who was admitted earlier would be taken there.'

'I don't know the sister,' the nurse said, 'but if you turn left and then take the lift to the next floor you'll see the sign directing you there.'

'Thank you.'

Walking on she felt a curious sense of disorientation as if her mission here were being elbowed out of the way by other thoughts, other half-remembered sentences that were springing into her mind.

'Sister Mary Concepta is sleeping and is as comfortable as may be expected.' A frosty faced nurse detained her at the door of the Intensive Care ward.

'Then it's not possible for me to see her? Shall I come back later or wait?'

'In a couple of hours.' The frosty face had melted into a prim little smile. 'She will probably be awake then and feeling more the thing.'

'Thank you.' Sister Joan retraced her footsteps to the van.

There was little sense in driving back to the convent and then returning. Mass was due to start at the parish church anyway. She walked briskly through the main gates and down the hill.

Father Stephens was celebrating the mass this morning which meant that Father Malone would be rushing off to the hospital the moment he heard about Sister Mary Concepta. She slipped into a rear pew and knelt, receiving a faint, enquiring smile from Sister Jerome who always slipped in after the priest had arrived on the altar as if she had been guarding the door in case he tried to run away.

The trouble with me, Sister Joan thought, fixing her mind firmly on the opening prayers is that I cannot live in a state of spiritual recollection. Stray thoughts jump in and out of my head like puppies in a dog basket. The evils of vivisection. Asking the way somewhere. Constable Brown. She lifted her rosary and held it tightly willing herself to concentrate.

'Good morning, Sister Joan. Is anything wrong at the convent?' Sister Jerome detained her as Father Stephens, having dismissed the Angel of the Presence, swept into the sacristy.

'Sister Mary Concepta was taken into hospital early this morning. It isn't as serious as we feared but I shall go back to the hospital later when she's awake.'

'Come and have some breakfast. I shall have some with you in the kitchen.'

The presbytery kitchen smelt of frying bacon and bread and resounded to the soft plopping of poached eggs.

'I'll just serve Father Stephens and then we can have ours,' Sister Jerome said, vanishing into the dining-room.

A few minutes later Sister Joan was eating her slice of dry brown bread, drinking a second coffee and peeling an apple in concert with her companion who observed, 'After so many

years on a light vegetarian diet I find it quite distasteful to have
to cook animal flesh. As for eating it!'

I could murder a nice crisp rasher of bacon, Sister Joan
thought, smiling a reply.

'I hope Sister Mary Concepta will soon be recovered.' Sister
Jerome looked worried.

'She's a tough old lady,' Sister Joan said. 'She and Sister
Gabrielle are engaged in a contest to see which one can outlast
the other. Doesn't it strike you as funny that we go on and on
about the joys of the life beyond the grave and then do every
mortal thing in our power to delay getting there?'

'It doesn't strike me as funny at all,' Sister Jerome said.
'Death isn't a subject for levity, Sister Joan. I was hearing only
yesterday at the grocer's shop of a most sad coincidence. The
woman who was found dead in the cemetery—'

'Mrs Rufus.'

'She met her death on the anniversary of her husband's
death,' Sister Jerome said.

Sister Joan sat bolt upright, a piece of apple suspended
halfway to her mouth.

'Are you sure, Sister?' she asked.

'I'm not in the habit of repeating unconfirmed gossip,' Sister
Jerome said. 'At least two ladies, as well as the grocer,
commented on the fact.'

'Sister Jerome, may I use the telephone?'

'Yes, of course, Sister. It's in Father Malone's study. You
know the way.'

'Thank you, Sister.'

Sister Joan went through into the hall and thence into the
shabby, familiar study with its shelves of books and piles of
parish magazines and the framed snapshots of Father Malone
on his pilgrimage tour to Lourdes, Santiago and Rome which
he had taken and frequently talked about to his parishioners.

'Mother Dorothy? Will you tell Sister Perpetua and the rest of
the community that Sister Mary Concepta's condition isn't as
serious as we feared? They want to keep her in for a few days to
be on the safe side, and I'm going back later this morning to see
her when she wakes up, but the news is very encouraging.'

'Thanks be to God! I'll tell the others immediately. Have you had anything to eat, Sister Joan?'

'I'm having some at the presbytery, Mother Dorothy.'

'Give our love to Sister Jerome.'

'Yes, of course. God bless.' Sister Joan replaced the receiver and immediately dialled the police station. 'Sister Joan here. Is Detective Sergeant Mill there?'

'He's not in yet,' Constable Brown's voice informed her without apology.

'Constable Brown, when the young woman came to the police station to make enquiries you told her that Detective Sergeant Mill was away, is that right?'

'Yes.'

'She came in and asked to speak to the officer in charge?'

'Yes. I told her that Detective Sergeant Mill wasn't in the building and offered my own assistance.'

'To answer her enquiries?'

'Yes. I don't quite see—'

'What enquiries did she make, Constable?'

'She asked the way to the convent,' Constable Brown said.

'That was all?'

'She asked the way to the convent and Constable Petrie who came in at that moment took her to the door and indicated the general direction she ought to take.'

'And you didn't record her question in the record book?'

'No, Sister. We don't record every trivial little enquiry in the book or we'd never be done writing up our notes.'

'She didn't report that her sister was missing?'

'No.'

'Constable, please bear with me.'

'Yes, Sister?' He sounded wearily patient.

'This young woman asked for directions to the convent? Did you tell Detective Sergeant Mill exactly what she wanted?'

'Detective Sergeant Mill never asked me exactly what was said,' Constable Brown said. 'I assumed that Constable Petrie had told him. Detective Sergeant Mill merely informed me that I ought to have noted the incident in the record book.'

'And you didn't say to him that she'd only asked for

directions?'

'No, Sister. I assumed he was aware of the tenor of the conversation already.'

'And you never thought of saying that it seemed rather unnecessary to have to record the fact that someone had come in to ask for directions?'

'It isn't my place to argue with the Detective Sergeant.'

'Thank you, Constable Brown.'

And God bless Policeman Plod, Sister Joan thought in exasperation, putting down the telephone.

Coming out of the study she met Father Stephens who greeted her in his usual rather gracious fashion.

'Sister Jerome tells me that Sister Mary Concepta is in the hospital. I trust she isn't too ill?'

'Not as ill as we feared, Father.'

'We must be thankful for that, though at Sister Mary Concepta's age death must seem much less daunting than it does to us.'

'Yes, Father,' Sister Joan said kindly, thinking of the two old ladies who most certainly were not prepared to go gentle into the good night.

'Thank you for the breakfast, Sister Jerome.' She went through into the kitchen.

'You're very welcome, Sister Joan. I expect we shall be kept informed of her progress?'

'Yes, of course, Sister. God bless.'

She went out, sidestepping Father Stephens who said as he put on his coat, 'The communion cup is excellent, Sister Joan. Father Malone will adore it when it's presented to him. Thank you.'

'You're welcome, Father.'

She escaped down the front path and turned in the direction of the hospital, though she doubted if Sister Mary Concepta would've woken up yet.

Things were slotting together in her mind now. There had been the misunderstanding between Detective Sergeant Mill and Constable Brown with the latter believing he had been given a light reprimand for not recording a request for directions while the former hadn't questioned what she herself had repeated after she'd spoken to Caroline. No, not Caroline but Crystal. Or was it so?

She had reached the narrow street known as Tor Alley. It was, she thought, inevitable that her footsteps should have led her here and now paused as if some invisible barrier stretched across the road preventing her from carrying straight on.

Perhaps the police were conducting a second search of the antique shop. She turned into the cobbled street and walked slowly past the hairdresser's establishment to the plate-glass windows with their carefully arranged treasures. A *Closed* notice hung inside the door and the window blinds were partly drawn down. Either Michael Peter had been arrested or was paying belated respects to the recently deceased Mrs Rufus. Harsh-voiced, sentimental Mrs Rufus who had merely happened to be in the wrong place at the wrong time.

Sister Joan walked on, rounding the corner of the building, entering the long narrow passage that ran down the side of the building to the extension at the back where the waxwork exhibition was housed.

The key that Michael Peter had given her was still in her pocket. She took it out as she reached the door and inserted it carefully into the lock, remembering to turn it twice and thus deactivate the alarm.

The staircase up which Michael Peter had hoped the feet of schoolchildren keen on acquiring knowledge of the past would tramp was dim and silent. It was quiet as if all the figures on the upper floor held their breaths.

Sister Joan began to climb the staircase, treading lightly, though her breath came short in her throat.

Upstairs she switched on the lights, bracing herself for the waxworks. There they were, in their tableaux, heads fixed at an angle that would never alter, eyes lowered, garments perfectly in character but motionless.

She walked swiftly past the funeral scene, the family outing – then struck by an unpleasant thought turned back briefly and looked more attentively at the first group of figures. She stepped over to the coffin and looked down at the fair-haired girl who lay with hands folded around a silken rose, eyes closed. The figure lay supine, and when she touched the cheek of the figure she felt a little shock of relief when her fingers touched cold wax.

She walked on slowly, catching her teeth in her lips with relief when she reached the first group of figures and opened the door beyond which the upper floor with its massive pieces of furniture stretched to the stairs that led down into the main shop.

This was foolish! She had come here because she had some notion that Crystal might be found here. Michael Peter adored his wife, adored her even though by now he must be regarding her as capable of murder. His dear old mother had probably drummed the notions of stiff upper lip and a gentleman's honour into him, so that whatever his wife or his wife's sister might have done would be regarded by him as something to be kept closely within the bounds of the family. That was why he'd gone to such lengths to pretend that Crystal hadn't left him, that she hadn't sneaked back and stolen from him. And that was why he hadn't mentioned in his statement that he'd lent Sister Joan a key to his premises that would enable her to get in and out unobserved. He wanted the murderer caught but he didn't want to be the one to point the finger.

She came down the stairs into the shop proper and looked round. If the police had been back to search the premises a second time they had been tactful about it. To her eyes she could see nothing different from the way it had all looked before.

It had been a mistake to come, she decided, one of those impulsive decisions best not acted upon. What on earth had she expected to find? The marble ashlar smeared with blood occupying pride of place among the various items for sale?

She walked to the front door and tried her key in the lock, but it failed to turn. Evidently it fitted only the back premises. That meant she would have to return the way she had come, a prospect that was decidedly unpleasing!

Better get it over with! With the disquieting feeling that she was in the wrong place at the wrong time she went back up the stairs and across the dimly lit room with its lurking dressers and Victorian wardrobes.

She went through into the extension, walking rapidly past the vapid-faced figures that set fires, bowled hoops, wheeled prams, flirted with military bucks at a ball and never moved onwards, past the funeral party with the open coffin and the little group of mourners.

Not all the mourners had been wearing black. The thought screamed into her mind as she reached the top of the staircase. There had been an extra white-clad figure that stood stiffly on the edge of the group.

She turned back, stepping noiselessly along the thick carpet and looked again at the white-gowned figure with the curly golden hair. Under the electric light the other figures, frozen into perpetual stillness, stared back at her. The white-clad one looked awkward and out of place like a guest wearing the wrong clothes at a party. Sister Joan stepped closer, put out her hand and gave the figure a little push. It swayed slightly, its eyes still closed. Not real then! Someone was playing games again.

Swinging about on her heel she looked at the coffin where the fair-haired figure lay, hands clasped about the stem of the silken rose. Her voice was pitched a shade higher as she said, 'You can get up now, Crystal!'

FOURTEEN

'You know then?' The fair-haired figure sat up, eyes wide and trusting. 'You know that I'm hiding from Caroline?'

'It was Caroline who married Michael Peter?'

'Pretending to be me.' The other sat up and began to climb down to the floor. 'I've been so frightened, Sister, not knowing what to do or where to go. She is very cunning, you know, very clever. Look what she did to me!'

She drew her hair aside to display a cut and swollen ear, with a handkerchief tied clumsily around it.

'That looks sore,' Sister Joan said.

'It bled and bled. Ears do, you know. It soaked the sweater and the skirt so naturally she had to take them off. Fortunately there was the long brown coat which hides a multitude of sins. This dress suits me better because it's white. White for purity.'

'Caroline wears brown,' Sister Joan said.

'She's a brown kind of person. Don't you think that she's a brown kind of person?'

'I don't know very much about Caroline at all,' Sister Joan said.

'She was always jealous of me. That was the trouble from the beginning,' the other said with a little sigh. 'I was always the pretty one, the one who was outgoing and lively and had plenty of friends – would have had plenty of friends if Caroline hadn't always followed me around, embarrassed me by being gauche and sullen. I tried not to mind, honestly. I was her kid sister and she was looking out for me, but that wasn't really the truth. The truth was that she couldn't ever make any friends of her own. There was something in her that made people back away. That's a terrible thing to say about a sister but it's true. It's something I've finally had to admit.'

'She was the one who stayed at home?'

'She had a part-time job, temping – her shorthand and typing were really quite competent, and then after Mum died Dad was really ill. Bad heart! Caroline stayed at home and was the dutiful daughter. I used to feel sorry for her, really I did. I had my own flat and lots of boyfriends and I used to get jobs as hostess at big conferences and trade fairs. I was always in demand.'

'What did Caroline do?' Sister Joan asked.

'She pretended to be me. Of course Dad didn't realize it at the time. Caroline got a job as hostess and met Michael Peter. He was middle-aged and lonely and not attractive to women so it was easy enough. She told him her name was Crystal and she married him under that name. Of course she couldn't very well ask Dad to the wedding! That would have given the whole game away. But once she got down here she started to worry in case I decided to turn up and then Michael Peter'd've known. She had to think of something so she went away to think. She went to see Dad, and then it occurred to her! She'd bring Dad down here and talk to him, try to make him understand why she had acted the way that she did. They walked over the moor together and went into the little chapel and she tried to explain to him but he wouldn't listen. He wouldn't listen, Sister! He became very agitated and then he clutched at his chest and said a tight band was choking him and died. She didn't know what on earth to do because if Dad was identified then it would all come out so she took everything she could find off him and crept back into the house and hid them in the centre of a toilet roll. If they were ever found then Michael Peter might've been blamed for causing Dad's death.'

'How did – she get into the house?'

'She had a key, of course, that deactivated the alarm. It was very easy to sneak in and leave the things there.'

'And then she came to me?' Sister Joan kept her voice soft.

'She didn't want to be married to Michael Peter any longer.

He's dull and boring and always going on about his stupid mother. If she just left him he'd never divorce her and he'd get to keep all the pretty ornaments. But if Michael Peter was sent to prison then she could come back and live in the house. And so she came to you.'

'But not to the police.'

'I asked a policeman – his name was Mill – or he said something about a Mill for directions to the convent. I know I told you that I'd gone to report my sister's death but they'd have investigated that, wouldn't they? And I didn't want to tell a big lie. I only tell white lies. So in the end I plucked up courage and asked you for help. Caroline asked you for help.'

'You're not Caroline?'

Sister Joan was edging away, her eyes on the other's face.

'I'm Crystal,' the girl said patiently. 'Caroline was only pretending to be me. I was missing according to her and she feared that Michael Peter might've done me some harm. But that didn't seem to be working, so Caroline decided there had to be a real murder. Mrs Rufus always went to the cemetery on the anniversary of her husband's death. She used to go very early in the morning to have a quiet time with her memories. Michael Peter told Crystal that. Told Caroline who was pretending to be Crystal.'

She shook her head slightly and a lock of her fair hair caught on a crust of dried blood on her earlobe.

'So Caroline stole the ashlar?'

'She sneaked in the house and took the marble ball and the pretty horse that stood on the sitting-room table and put them very carefully in the wheelie bag that Mrs Rufus kept in the pantry and wheeled them away. When Mrs Rufus went to the cemetery on Monday morning Caroline met her there and told her that it was her father who lay in the unmarked grave, and Mrs Rufus came over and bent down and the rest was easy. She was a very trusting woman, as trusting as Crystal. It isn't wise to trust people or love them too much. Don't you agree, Sister?'

'Crystal loved Caroline?' Sister Joan ventured.

'Crystal adored Caroline.' The girl gave another deeper sigh. 'She tried very hard to be kind to her, to get her to wear pretty things and use make-up. She used to say "You're not much older than I am, Caro. Get yourself a life!" She even tried to get Caroline interested in the animal rights cause. Too too boring! You can guess what Caroline did the minute she married Michael Peter!'

'Persuaded him to buy a jacket for her with real sable cuffs?'

'Exactly! It wouldn't fit in the case when she left but she knew she could always come back and get it later on. The problem was that nobody was connecting the unknown man in the chapel with Michael Peter at all. So Caroline went back and buried a strip of paper with his name and telephone number on it, but the police didn't make a second search and I don't think that he's been arrested for Mrs Rufus's death yet either.'

'The law can work very slowly sometimes.'

She had moved almost imperceptibly to the next tableau. The crinolined ladies at the ball sat with fans suspended, their heads tilted coquettishly.

'Most people are stupid,' the girl said. 'Even Caroline can be foolish sometimes. Mrs Rufus bled, you see. The blood sprayed up out of the back of her head like a red fountain and went all over the sweater and skirt. It was lucky she had taken off her coat or that would've been soaked too. She put it back on and walked up to the place where she was staying.'

'The little schoolhouse.'

'She hurt Crystal then. She took a sharp knife that was meant for cutting bread and she slashed at her ear. She slashed at my ear, Sister, and it bled and bled and mixed with the blood that Mrs Rufus had sprayed. It was all over the skirt and the sweater so she took them off and stuffed them in the boot of the old car, and put a wedge to hold the boot open a bit, in case someone missed them. They were proof against Michael Peter, don't you see? Then she put on the brown coat and tied a scarf over her head and took a train to the next town and bought a lovely white dress and stayed the night in an hotel there. That was rather clever of her actually. People were out looking for someone who was hiding out in a barn or on the moor and all the time she was sitting in a very respectable hotel room, not being noticed by anybody at all.'

'And where is Caroline now?' Sister Joan asked.

'I don't know. That's what scares me so.' The eyes were wide and anxious. 'I hid here because I hoped that you might come to search by yourself. The newspaper article said that you worked on hunches and so I just prayed that you'd come and find me before she did. The police were here when I arrived so I just wandered off down the alley and sat on a bench until they went. Then I let myself in. Michael Peter gave Caroline a key ages ago but she never used it. I deactivated the alarm so that you could get in more easily. You won't let Caroline get me again, will you?'

'What exactly did Caroline do to Crystal?' Sister Joan asked.

'She pushed me under a train,' the other said. 'It was rush hour and very crowded and nobody saw what really happened. Sometimes I think that perhaps Caroline didn't really mean to do it. She loved me, you see. She absolutely adored me! Even when she was wishing she was me – but that's a form of adoration too, isn't it, Sister? Dad was so upset! He acted as if he'd lost the only daughter he had. Well, he adored her more than anyone in the world, you know. He didn't seem to notice that Caroline was still alive, that it was Caroline who stayed home when Mum died and helped in the house and ran his errands and took him over to the Heart Unit when he was due for treatment. Caroline did all that but he only ever talked about me, how I cared so much for poor dumb creatures.'

'Perhaps Caroline has gone for good,' Sister Joan said.

'Oh, she'll come back if she can.' The other tugged at her fair hair. 'She won't stay hid for long. When I make a friend she comes out of hiding then and spoils it all for me. My ear stings so. It bled and bled.'

The golden curls were slipping sideways, catching on the crusted blood, then breaking free in a cascade of flaxen ringlets.

'Well,' said the girl, looking at the wig in her hand, 'that's enough of that nonsense! I'm here looking for my sister Crystal. She's somewhere around. Always in the back of my head. Always worrying about my lack of a social life, always urging me to strike out on my own as if I could just walk out on

Dad. She hardly ever visited you see. Once a month was a record for her! And when she did condescend to float in it was, "And what has my beautiful daughter been doing with herself lately? Caro, get a cup of coffee for your sister! Hurry up! Crystal can't stay long". And I'd make the coffee and nobody noticed if I brought in three cups or two. But nothing was said. Nothing was ever said. You liked Crystal, didn't you, Sister? You liked my sister better than you like me. People always do.'

'I never met her,' Sister Joan said, dry mouthed.

'She isn't really dead,' Caroline said. 'She's in my head, right at the back. She likes to come out now and then. But she's scared of me. Isn't that odd? My own little sister is afraid of me. Are you scared of me, Sister?'

'No,' said Sister Joan. 'No, I'm not scared of you.'

'Then you're a fool,' Caroline said. 'You like Crystal better than you like me. I know that. I want someone to like me. Mrs Rufus didn't like me. She thought that I'd married Crystal's husband for his money.'

'Michael Peter is your husband.'

'Oh, don't be so stupid!' The wig was tossed to the floor. 'Do you think that I'd really marry an old fogy like that? It was Crystal who married him and serve her right! She had loads of men friends – lovers I think – though you'd never get Dad to believe it! It served her right to be landed with Michael Peter! I got to live in the pretty house and wear the expensive clothes but she had to put up with his fumbling after the lights were switched off! I knew she wouldn't be able to endure it for ever but in the end she wasn't around any longer. There was just me in that lonely place with that housekeeper woman complaining because I liked pop music and when there was nothing to do I used to paint my nails. I thought that if I did that then Crystal might come back but she stayed away and I was worried about Dad, by himself in the new flat and writing to enquire when was I going to visit him? So I went to see Dad and brought him to the chapel. 'What on earth are we doing here, Caroline? And why have we had to walk such a long way? Why not get a taxi? What the devil's going on?" So I told him that I was really Crystal disguised as Caroline and that Caroline had pushed me under the train. And he began to sweat and gasp and I just stood there looking at him and thinking that now there might be a way to get that wretched old fogy that Crystal had married indicted for murder or something. Crystal was coming back soon you see, and before she comes I get muddled in the head sometimes. But that didn't stop you liking her, did it, Sister?'

In another moment she would snap and run screaming down the long carpet past the stiffly poised waxwork figures. Not all stiffly poised! Out of the corner of her eye she caught a movement as a tall officer slid silently from his position, and rocked slightly as a figure stepped out from behind.

'Caroline Peter?' said Detective Sergeant Mill.

'I'm looking for my sister. I'm looking for Crystal,' she said.

'I think you'd better give me that bread knife, don't you?' He sounded cool as ice.

'It's Crystal's.' She dropped it on the carpet and shivered. 'Crystal uses that.'

'Caroline Peter, I'm arresting you for the murder of Mary Rufus. You don't have to say anything—'

The routine warnings were given. Sister Joan heard the snap of handcuffs as Constable Brown stepped from behind another figure. The young woman in the white dress stood very still. Then she raised her head and said anxiously, 'I'm looking for my sister Crystal. She got married last year and we haven't heard a word from her since Easter.'

Constable Whitney came through the door and bent to pick up the knife and slide it into a plastic bag.

'Get that to the lab. boys, Constable.' Detective Sergeant Mill nodded at him. 'Come and sit down for a minute, Sister. You look a trifle shaken up.'

'I didn't know she had a knife,' Sister Joan said, taking the proffered chair. 'It was tucked through the sash and hidden by the folds of the gown. If I'd realized that – I don't think that I'd ever have come here.'

'Why did you come?' he enquired.

'Impulse – instinct – I don't know.' She shrugged slightly. 'I've been racking my brains about all this and there comes a point when you have to stop reasoning things out and begin acting as the spirit moves. I had kept the key that Michael Peter gave me, and I think that subconsciously I knew that I'd need to use it again sometime. And this was the logical place for her to come, wasn't it? After it had been searched?'

'Yes.' He pulled up another chair and sat down, his expression serious and thoughtful. 'Did you know that Crystal, the real Crystal, was dead when you came?'

'I'm not that heroic,' Sister Joan said wryly. 'I did guess that she wasn't the original Crystal when the specialist at the hospital mentioned having treated John Hayes and of having met his daughter Crystal who was an animal rights activist. There was a jacket with sable cuffs in the suitcase that Michael Peter threw away, and I knew that anyone keen on animal rights would never have worn it. I thought Crystal might be back in London. Then when I saw the figure in the coffin I thought it wiser to go along and address her as Crystal. How did you—'

'You applied to St Catherine's House for their birth certificates.'

'To make sure there were really two sisters.'

'What you didn't know,' he said, 'and what we only recently found out was that Crystal Hayes died eighteen months ago. She fell on to the line in front of an approaching train. It was rush hour and nobody saw clearly what had happened. The coroner brought in a verdict of accident.'

'And Caroline couldn't deal with the fact that the sister she both adored and hated was dead. She had to make her alive again. She had to give Crystal a wealthy husband and a beautiful house. But it was Caroline who had to put up with the husband and live in the house. I think she decided to confess and brought her father down originally to do that, but somewhere along the way she decided to tell him privately. He was in bad health. There was the possibility the shock might kill him, and then she could tie it up to Michael Peter and – but where has she been since Easter?'

'I'd wager she's been living as Caroline, helping her father to move house, blocking any queries that might come from her husband down here in Cornwall. But her father got the message that Michael Peter had left at the Heart Unit and then she probably decided to bring him down here. He must've been under the impression that they were coming to beard Michael in his lair. Who knows how her mind was working or what she said?'

'She enlisted me on her side,' Sister Joan said.

'Very cleverly too. She's very intelligent and very cunning. I've no doubt she read the newspaper article some time before and kept it in mind. She went to the station and asked for directions to the convent, so in that way she could block your insisting she went to the police. If Brown had actually informed me that he hadn't recorded her request because she had only asked the way somewhere then we'd have been a whole lot further forward but Brown didn't repeat the conversation verbatim and I assumed that he was talking about her reporting her sister missing – that's a lesson to me not to assume too readily!'

'But it wouldn't have saved Mrs Rufus?'

'I don't think so.' He shook his head slightly. 'Caroline had made up her mind that Mrs Rufus had to go. You know the poor woman probably went and put the flowers on her husband's grave and then went over to look at the unmarked grave and decided to leave a few flowers there. And Caroline came up behind and smashed the ashlar down on her head.'

'That wasn't what she told me.'

'She wanted to display how clever she was to lure Mrs Rufus to the grave, but the housekeeper would've recognized her and started asking questions. She wouldn't have turned her back and knelt down. We found the ashlar by the way. In the wheelie bag along with the T'ang horse under the desk in the outer office. She intended it to implicate Michael Peter. Then with him safely locked away in jail she could turn up again as Crystal with some excuse for her long absence and take over the house and the business. If you're feeling all right now, Sister, I'll drive you home.'

'I'm feeling fine and I have to go up to the hospital to see if Sister Mary Concepta is better yet. Alan, what will happen to her now?'

'She'll be found unfit to plead and placed in a secure mental hospital. There won't be any trial, Sister.'

'And in the end she came here.' Sister Joan looked round at the silent waxy figures and shivered. 'When she first pretended to be Crystal she kept her own appearance, so why the wig?'

'Because only Crystal could tell what had really happened on that railway station? The human mind is a peculiar thing, Sister.'

'Some would call it conscience,' Sister Joan said, and stopped suddenly as they moved towards the back stairs. 'How did you get here? Were you here all the time?'

'When you tried to open the front door with the back-door key you triggered an alarm that rang down in the station,' he said. 'We were here within a couple of minutes. Even the police can move silently when it's necessary. And we had the key to the front door.'

'God bless the police,' Sister Joan said fervently as they went down the stairs.

It had been an excellent surprise. Father Malone had accepted the chalice with a beaming face and the children had clapped enthusiastically when he had promised to show them his photographs of his pilgrimage to Lourdes, Santiago and Rome. He had also expressed warm thanks to Mr Michael Peter for selling the chalice at such a generous price. It was unfortunate that Mr Peter had locked up house and shop and put both on the market, prior to travelling abroad for his health.

Sister Joan drove back to the convent feeling that pleasant things ought to happen more often. It was full summer now and very hot. The town water supply was said to be threatened by the drought and there was talk of standpipes. There was always talk of standpipes if the summer lasted for longer than a fortnight.

The grass was browning at the tips and the air had a scorching dusty feeling. The van windows were open but the steering wheel felt hot and sticky. She slowed down as she neared the old schoolhouse, her spirits rising further as she saw a familiar figure tinkering with the old car.

'Brother Cuthbert, you're back!'

Scrambling down from the van she hurried towards him.

'Like a thief in the night, Sister! How are you? The door was open so I simply walked in. Isn't it glorious weather?'

He shook hands, his freckled young face flushed with heat and pleasure.

'Some wouldn't agree, but I like the heat,' Sister Joan said. 'They allowed you to return here then?'

'Father Superior said that as I was so useless as a member of the community I might as well stay down here and concentrate on my spiritual life,' Brother Cuthbert said. 'It chimed so well with my own wishes that I felt quite guilty! But another year or two may bring me maturity, don't you think? And prayer rises up so readily here where the moors stretch to the sky. How are you, Sister? And the other dear Sisters?'

'Sister Mary Concepta had a short spell in hospital and is home again now. The rest of us are well. There was someone staying in the schoolhouse while you were away. It's a long story.'

'To do with evil?' Brother Cuthbert looked uncomfortable.

'As a matter of fact, yes.'

'Evil only exists where there is a complete absence of good,' Brother Cuthbert said.

'But you sensed evil?'

'I sensed confusion,' Brother Cuthbert said. 'A mind turned against itself. A love twisted into hatred. Don't worry, Sister. I'll air the place with a few Hail Marys and a couple of Paternosters. Evil never lasts.'

'And hatred?' she queried.

'The other side of adoration,' Brother Cuthbert said cheerfully. 'God knows which side of the coin to judge! Are they all well in town? I did call at the presbytery but everybody was out.'

'At a presentation at the children's home. I'll tell you about it later.'

'And that very nice police officer?' He thought an instant, then clicked his fingers. 'Detective Sergeant Mill! Nice fellow.'

'He's very well.'

'He absolutely adores you,' Brother Cuthbert said. 'When I think of you two I think of Saint Francis and Saint Clare, sister and brother in Christ.'

'Good heavens!' Sister Joan said faintly, vainly trying to picture Detective Sergeant Mill in the role of that pantheistic saint.

'Not that he'd admit it, of course,' Brother Cuthbert said, strolling back with her to the van. 'He's an agnostic, isn't he?'

'Somewhat!'

'Agnostics are people who haven't found the right road,' Brother Cuthbert said. 'What a blessing you must be to him!'

'I'll tell him some time. God bless.'

Climbing back behind the hot and sticky wheel she waited until she had driven a little way out of earshot before she allowed herself to laugh. She was still chuckling as she drove though the convent gates, all evil fled away and the hot sun blazing.

07-99

F   Black, Veronica
        A vow of adoration

GAYLORD FG